For Helen Turner and Margaret Mahy,
who both seemed to be from New Zealand

MARY HOFFMAN

SPECIAL POWERS

BARN OWL BOOKS

The author acknowledges
Professor Michio Kaku's Hyperspace *(OUP, 1994)*
as the inspiration behind the explanation
about higher dimensions on pages 51-54.

BARN OWL BOOKS
157 Fortis Green Road, London, N10 3LX

First Published in 1997 by Hodder Children's Books

This edition Barn Owl Books, 2008
157 Fortis Green Road, London, N10 3LX

Distributed by Frances Lincoln,
4 Torriano Mews, Torriano Avenue, London, NW5 2RZ

ISBN 978 1 903015 78 0

Front cover images © histvan/coka,Shutterstock
Designed and typeset by Skandesign Limited
Printed in the UK by Cox and Wyman

Contents

1

By any other name

I took the box down from the wardrobe and lifted out some old essays. Underneath them was a notebook, with astrological symbols on the cover. I had never seen it before, but when I opened it, I saw the white pages were covered in my handwriting. It was dated three years ago, back in the time when I was still Emily. I started to read...

I like to think it was my parents' fault. If they'd only given me a more interesting name I might not have spent so much time fantasising about alternative lives. I agree you can't do *much* when you're stuck with Grey as a surname – it's a bit of a downer. But they could have tried Catriona or Esmerelda or Arianwen. I mean, there are even people called Magic or Tallulah or Cherish. I found out two years ago that my great grandmother on my father's side was called Sidonia! And what did they choose? Emily. Emily Grey.

You think you've heard of her. You haven't, but she sounds like a character in a Jane Austen novel, doesn't she? Something you've seen dramatised on BBC2. Not the spunky heroine of course. A walk-on part in a minor scene, a dull, plain, ladylike, obedient wimp. Emily Grey would definitely wear a bonnet.

From the time I could understand anything at all, I knew I hated my name. It wasn't just that it was a dull and ordinary-sounding name; what I really hated was that it turned me into the person I imagined the name fitted. I've always wanted to be daring and swashbuckling, someone who *does* things and has adventure. But does this sound right? 'Emily Grey the pirate was the terror of the seven seas.' Or this? 'Today we have an interview with intrepid mountaineer, Emily Grey.' Try this: 'Miss Emily Grey will be the first woman astronaut to captain her own space probe.' No. Emily Grey is a quiet bank clerk, a woman who lives with her elderly aunt, has lots of cats and does knitting. The closest she gets to an adventure is changing her library book. Actually that's one thing I do have in common with the other Emily, the one I'm afraid I might become. I love the library. I've never understood why people think librarians are boring, Emily Grey sort of people. The two in my local library aren't like that at all.

There's Joel, who's drop-dead gorgeous. He's six foot tall, thin, with long brown hair in a ponytail, and he always has a book closed on his finger at the page where he's stopped reading, even when he's stamping other people's books out. He has a dreamy faraway look in his gorgeous big eyes (and the longest eyelashes you ever saw on a man) and a small half-smile on his beautiful mouth. Sigh! Oh yes, and the other one's Isis. She's about the same height as Joel, slim and black and with a wonderful cascade of shiny plaits fountaining from the top of her head. My friend Daniella says they're extensions but I think she's just being bitchy. Daniella has short frizzy hair that just won't grow long, however hard she tugs it.

Anyway, Joel and Isis were my two favourite people, till I met Archie. I used to dream about being older and sharing a flat with Isis. We'd drink lots of coffee and red wine and not bother much about food. But we'd have overflowing bookshelves, really interesting breakfast-conversations about books, the fascinating bits of plots and the names of characters like Lyra Belacqua, Prince Caspian, Arwen Evenstar. (Breakfast chat at home was usually limited to stuff like 'Have you got your games kit, Emily?' or 'Don't forget your violin, Emily').

My other fantasy was that one day Joel would notice me, me properly as another human on the same planet as him, and ask me out. I bet he *would* have noticed me if my library ticket had said 'Arwen'.

Anyway, the closest I ever got to either was that Isis was really friendly and good at recommending the sort of books I like. She introduced me to Diana Wynne Jones, Margaret Mahy and Robin McKinley. And, come to think of it, Joel *did* know who I was, because he suggested I try Terry Pratchett and Ann McCaffrey. As you can probably tell, I'm a complete fantasy freak.

It's really only in the library that I stop being Emily Grey, because I get all these books there that let me step into my other life. The one where I'm tall and impressive, not shortish and average. Where I wear magnificent flowing robes and jewels and have unlimited powers of sorcery and enchantment. I generally have an army too, and a whole fleet of servants. Frequently I have a tame panther or cheetah who adores me and obeys my every word. I've had violet eyes and red hair and a figure to kill for. I've ruled continents and kingdoms and had emperors and tyrants begging on their knees for mercy. I talk to dragons and control the weather…

This isn't exactly how it is in any particular books I've read, though they do give me lots of ideas. It's a sort of mixture of all my favourite bits. This is how I am in my head, the *real* me that other people don't know. My sensible parents think I'm their sensible daughter, bookish and quiet. My teachers think I'm a steady plodder, a regular B-plusser in all subjects, a bit hopeless at games, but useful on the school magazine. My friends, well, I haven't got many. Daniella was the best, till Archie came along. But I'm getting ahead of myself. What none of these people know is that I'm really K'sedra, Empress-Mage of the Desert Kingdom of Krin or whoever I happen to be at the time (K'sedra is my favourite). They see only Emily Grey who is ordinary, ordinary, ordinary. But the real me is special and can do all sorts of things they never dream of.

The first time I saw Archie was in Oak Grove library. She was just suddenly *there*, in the Fantasy section. I don't mean she materialised or was transported there, at least, I didn't think that then. At the time, I assumed she'd just come in quietly. She was riffling through the Dragonvale books to see if they had the latest one. They did, but it was at home under my pillow. I was rationing myself to a chapter a day, to make it last (it wasn't working because I often cheated and read two or more at bedtime).

'Are you looking for *Blood of the Kings*?' I asked. She looked surprised, and when she answered, spoke with an accent I couldn't quite place.

'The last Dragonvale book? Yes, I am,' she said.

'Well, the latest,' I said. 'I hope it won't be the last.'

'You are a fan?' asked the girl.

'Massive!' I answered. And then we were away. I'd always wanted a friend like her. One you could talk to about the things that *really* mattered, like the velvet hangings for a royal bedchamber or the number of priests you'd need in a procession to celebrate the Festival of the Spring Sacrifice. You couldn't talk to Daniella about that kind of thing; she only ever read High School Musical or Louise Rennison. She was full of opinions on hairstyles and clothes and bands but she couldn't understand the inner life of an Empress-Mage. It was strange that we were friends at all really, but we'd known each other since nursery school and now we lived in the same street, so we always walked to school together. She was a comfortable sort of best friend to have, but I was ready for someone a bit more exotic. And here she was, standing in the Fantasy section, with her finger in a closed copy of *The Ruby Knight* – like a female version of Joel.

She was taller than me (Most people are) and had that lovely rich chestnutty brown hair that always shines and never looks greasy. She was slim and casually dressed but still gave the impression that her clothes were carefully chosen. She had sparkly hazel sort of eyes that brought her face alive and she laughed a lot. Bags of self-confidence, that's what Archie had. When she told me her name I immediately wanted to know what it was short for. She seemed a bit awkward about answering.

'Promise not to laugh?' she asked.

'OK. Sure.' I said. 'I like unusual names, the more unusual the better.'

'I got teased so much in Primary school that I shortened it. My full name's Archway.'

Archway! Can you imagine anything more mysterious and intriguing?

'No kidding,' I said, full of respect.

'Yeah,' said Archie. 'The kids used to call me No-way and Way-out and all sorts of stuff.'

'I think it's wonderful,' I said hastily. 'What made your parents think of it?'

Archie looked uneasy. 'All my family have unusual names,' she said. I think that was when I knew I had a new best friend.

That was the Autumn half-term. Archie told me her family had just arrived from New Zealand and, joy of joys, she'd be starting at my school after the break. I vaguely remembered Daniella wittering on about a new girl and wondering what she'd be like, but I'd been busy marshalling my bodyguard of desert warriors to defend me against the beserkers of Krin at the time and hadn't paid her much attention.

Isis practically had to kick us out of the library (which closes early on Thursdays now because of council cuts), so we wandered off down the High Street towards the Coffee Bean café, where we carried on our conversation about books over chocolate milk-shakes.

Archie didn't seem to know what to order or quite how to drink it when it came. 'Don't you get milk-shakes in New Zealand?' I asked. Her bright hazel eyes made the same little shifting movement I'd noticed earlier.

'We lived right out in the country on a farm,' she said slowly. 'No cafés or restaurants or anything like that. Just a post-office, a school and a church.'

'What about a library?' I said, appalled at this image of cultural wilderness she was conjuring up.

'We had a sort of travelling one,' she said.

'Oh, a mobile.' I must have pulled a face, thinking of Lark Hill Forest's mobile library, a van full of large print romances for old ladies and tatty little hardbacks for kids, because she hurriedly added:

'It was a good one. They have to be in the country, and we always had lots of books in the house. It was my grandmother's house. Henrietta Power, you know – she's a writer.'

My first thought that Henrietta wasn't a particularly unusual name was blown away by the explosion of glory at Archie's having a real writer in her family. It didn't occur to me to wonder where Archie had got her Dragonvale books and other fantasies from. Her granny wasn't likely to have written that kind of book and the New Zealand mobile library must have been thousands of times better than ours if it could feed a serious fantasy habit. But I didn't think too hard about it because I was well on the way to becoming completely bewitched by the Power family, even though I'd only met one of them.

So, when Archie asked if I'd like to come over to her house at the weekend, I was thrilled. My parents didn't mind. Going to visit a girl who would be joining my class next week was just the polite, helpful sort of thing they approved of. But they did want to know things like what Archie's parents did for a living, questions I couldn't answer.

'Her grandmother's a writer,' I said proudly, tasting the two syllables on my tongue. My father, who is an accountant (Mr Grey the accountant, Miss Grey the accountant's daughter) made a little noise that sounded like a snort. He can be *so* contemptuous of anything unusual or creative.

'That's nice, dear,' said my mother, in her not-really-listening-to-you voice, which was all we ever seemed to hear since she'd started her evening classes.

The Powers were renting a big house in Avenue Road. It was red brick, covered in ivy and had pointed windows like a Gothic church. The road was full of houses with peculiar architectural details: iron weather-vanes, pierced stonework balconies, fancy chimney-pots and suchlike. I'd always like walking along it and now at last I had a reason to go into one of those houses. They looked as if they'd be stuffed with mysterious attics, unexplored corners, secret rooms and all sorts of hidden delights. Our house was square and modern and you could see everything there was to see at first glance.

Archie was standing, appropriately, in the pointed porch of her house, looking out for me. That was a good start. The hallway was full of packing cases, but there were already interesting pictures on the walls and a big blue vase overflowing with golden chrysanthemums, standing on one of the largest crates. A delicious smell of coffee wafted through from the back of the house. (I hate coffee and don't know how people can put it in their mouths but the *smell* is so evocative, sort of grown-up and *worldly*.)

A tall woman with long dark hair loose around her

shoulders came out of the shadows. She was really beautiful, with prominent cheekbones and winged eyebrows. Her face was hawk-like and alert, more my idea of a Native North American than a New Zealander. She was wearing long floaty clothes in autumn colours; there was definitely silk involved and perhaps even a bit of velvet. She didn't look a bit like a housewife unpacking a new home. She looked like a Empress-Mage, or, at least, an Empress-Mage's mother.

'This is Emily Grey, mother,' said Archie. 'Emily, this is my mother, Lisle.' (She pronounced it 'Lyle', but I could just hear that French 's' in the way it was spelt.)

'Emma Leigh,' said Lisle slowly, coming forward and taking my hand in both of hers. 'Good to see you. Welcome to our home.'

At the same moment as my glorious rechristening as Emma Leigh, an even lovelier vision than Archie's mother came down the stairs. A young man with a shock of dark curly hair, wearing jeans and an embroidered velvet waistcoat, descended into view, flashing me a gorgeous white smile as he loped out the front door.

'That was Fitzroy, my brother,' said Archie as I stood looking hungrily after him. 'We call him Fitz.' That was the moment I fell in love with the whole Power family, just as I had thought I would. Fitz was starting in the sixth form at my school on Monday too. I knew for certain that Daniella was going to be interested in the new girl as soon as she knew she had an older brother. And what a brother! He looked like Prince Khalid, leader of the rival faction in K'sedra's desert kingdom, a dashing piratical sort of figure. I just couldn't imagine him in the cafeteria of Elm Park School.

Lisle interrupted my daydream and swept me into the living room where she opened long wooden window shutters to let the golden autumn light in. She was asking my opinion on the dried-flower arrangement in the empty fireplace, when in came Archie's grandmother, followed by her father carrying a tray of coffee, hot chocolate and biscuits (I was really glad to see the chocolate, although by this time I'd have cheerfully swallowed arsenic at Lisle's bidding).

Henrietta Power looked like a grey-haired version of Lisle, which was odd, because she was Lisle's mother-in-law. I was completely over-awed by her, because she wrote books. She wore her hair in a pony-tail (I've *never* seen anyone with grey hair do that) and sticking out of the scrunchie that held it together were two pencils and a pen!

Portland Power, as he was introduced to me, looked like a Viking explorer. He was built on a large scale and had red-gold hair and a vigorous beard of the same colour. I was a bit scared of him; he looked strong and capable of great violence. But he put the tray down gently on the floor (they had no table) and shook my hand. His hands were surprisingly smooth and well-shaped for someone who looked as if he'd be more at home sailing the Atlantic single-handed, or perhaps strangling a bear.

There was a moment when they first came in, just an instant, when a quick glance was exchanged among the Powers and I felt a definite tingle in the room. 'This is a sort of test,' I thought, and wondered whether I would pass it. It wasn't until much later that I realised they were the ones on trial.

2

Standing out

If I had sat down at my desk and *designed* an interesting family for myself I couldn't have come up with anything better than the Powers. A daughter my age to be like a sister to me (I'm an only child, did I say? Emily Grey would be), a son who looked like the sort of person who should be on a poster on someone's wall, and exotic-looking mother and father and a grandmother who was a writer. That, plus their Addams-family-cum-Bohemian house would have been enough, but there were two uncles as well, Portland's younger twin brothers, Grosvenor and Albemarle, who lived in their attic – I knew that house would have an attic.

Grosvenor was a painter (those were his pictures in the hall) and Albemarle was a professional musician, a solo flute-player who would be giving some recitals in London. They were both tall and a bit shy, with the same curly hair as Fitz's, but red like Portland's. I never did find out exactly what Archie's parents did, except that they were associated with Lark Hill University while they were here. It never occurred to me to ask who was running the farm in New Zealand.

As a matter of fact I didn't *want* too much information about them. They were like characters in one of my favourite novels, intriguing by name and exotic in appearance, with vague and mysterious lives containing grand and impressive activities which didn't have to be specific as long as they were different from anything my parents did. I didn't want to think of their paying bills or scrambling eggs or brushing their teeth. Mind you, whenever I *did* stumble across them doing something ordinary and domestic, they always managed to be doing it in a way that invested it with glamour.

That first day, Portland had to go to the supermarket for groceries and asked Archie and me to help. I'm an absolute expert at the Sainsbury's weekly shop, from lettuces to lemonade. Down those mean aisles I've walked behind many a trolley, dreaming of the collapse of Empires and the deaths of poets. But I didn't need to retreat into the desert kingdom while shopping with Archie and her father.

For a start, we went in their camper-van. They didn't have an ordinary car, only this amazing pink Bedford with psychedelic patterns all over it. We all squeezed in and my eyes must have grown round at the sight of the inside of it because Portland smiled and asked, 'You like our little home from home, Emma Leigh?'

Like it? It was absolute magic. Did you ever have a doll's house or a toy shop when you were little? That was what the Power's van was like inside. Everything folded away and was perfectly designed to make the maximum use of space without looking clinical. It was a cross between a Romany caravan, a picnic hamper and the Egyptian room at Harrods. The Powers had driven all the way from New Zealand in it, supplementing the bunk beds with tents as they'd traversed continents and ferried their way across oceans. Even though there was nothing like it in the desert kingdom of Krin, I immediately adored it and wanted to travel the world in it too.

As we pulled into the Sainsbury's car-park a small clump of open-mouthed Lark Hill Foresters stood staring at us. The van was pretty incongruous, like a knickerbockers glory on a tray of rice-puddings. I immediately felt more special and Emma Leigh-ish; no one had *ever* stared at me in the car-park when I'd got out of our Volvo (grey, of course). Portland must have read my mind.

'Well, Emma Leigh,' he said, in that strange accent they all had. 'You'll have to help us out here. It's our first experience of a British supermarket.'

'I expect they're much the same the world over,' I said, blushing. The idea of my helping this golden berserker to select groceries struck me as deeply incongruous. As he grabbed a trolley in his large shapely hands I was briefly reminded of General Borghul, the leader of my army in the desert kingdom and the way he grasped the reins of his silver war-stallion. I shook my head. No need for the kingdom of Krin today.

'Now then,' said Portland. 'Salad!'

He might as well have uttered 'Ambrosia!' for all his shopping had to do with the cling-wrapped Icebergs and boxes of tomatoes my family usually bought. Lollo Rosso, radicchio, endive, rocket – all were tossed into the trolley. Vine tomatoes, a black pepper, salsify, alfalfa and avocadoes followed. My parents tended to think that celery was a bit daring. I dreaded to think what their bill was going to be at the checkout.

By the time we got there, we had a second trolley, and the shelves had been stripped of chanterelles, olive bread, tofu, couscous, seaweed, halva, balsamic vinegar, kumquats and lots of other things that had never found their way into the Grey weekly shopping basket. No meat or fish, though. The Powers were strict vegetarians. Even that struck me as fabulously appropriate, though my heart sank as I imagined what would happen if I brought Archie home for a meal. ('Would you like an omelette, dear? A cheese salad?') I thrust the image of lettuce, tomato, grated cheddar and salad cream from my mind and filled it with the dates and figs and almonds that K'sedra always kept piled high in silver dishes on her low intaglio tables.

'Well, that should keep the fox from the gate,' said Portland as we trundled the trolleys out through the first lot of doors. It didn't sound quite right but before I could think why, Archie grabbed my arm.

'Isn't that Isis?' It was. She was pinning a poster to the community notice-board. Archie dragged Portland and me over, trolleys and all, and introduced Portland to the beautiful librarian as if she had known her for years, instead of two days. Seeing my old and new idols together gave me a kind of trembly feeling, which was not entirely pleasant. I wanted them to like one another but I had a horrible feeling that if they did, there would be no space for me.

'I can't expect you to take much interest in local affairs yet, Mr Power,' Isis was saying. 'But I know Emily will want to get involved.' She turned to me and it was only then that I saw the red letters on the poster: SAY NO TO LIBRARY CLOSURE!

'What?' I said stupidly. 'What library?'

Isis gave Portland the kind of look patrons reserve for when their protégés play bum notes. 'Listen to her! Oak Grove of course! That's why I'm putting up these notices. We're having a meeting next week.'

'Close *our* library?' I said, still giving a good impression of being several sandwiches short of a picnic. I just couldn't take it in. It was like someone saying there weren't going to be any more Fridays or that red had been outlawed. But if I looked knocked sideways, Archie and her father looked even more appalled. Portland was actually stammering with rage.

'That's absolutely pr-pr-preposterous!' he exploded. Archie gave him a worried look. He was gripping the trolley as if it were the throat of a professional library closer. 'Ph-philistines!' he said. 'Wh-where is this meeting? We'll be there, you can count on it!' He grabbed the leaflet from Isis and stormed out of the exit towards the amazing technicolour dream van. Isis raised her eyebrows at me. She couldn't say much in front of Archie but she clearly thought Portland was a nutter, even though he might prove to be a useful one.

'Good to see someone who cares,' she said tactfully. 'See you both at the meeting?'

'You bet,' said Archie, accelerating her trolley after her retreating father. I only had time to nod and run after

27

them. Portland had wrenched open the back of the van and was hurling vegetables into it with no regard for their safety. 'Let's stack the shopping properly, Dad,' said Archie, 'Emily will think we don't know how to do things.' Portland sighed and stopped frowning.

Later I tried to get my parents to take an interest in what Isis had said about the library. Dad was slightlly annoyed. He was a regular, three-books-a-week man, with a slightly startling preference in such a mild person, for American thrillers. But he worked near the central library and could easily transfer his allegiance there.

'But it's a nuisance for you Emily, I can see,' he said. 'I'll come to the meeting if you like.'

It was a lot less than an enraged and spluttering Viking, but it was a lot more than I had expected.

'What about you, Mum?' I asked.

'It's difficult for the council,' she said unexpectedly. 'I don't suppose that they *want* to close the library, but they're forced into making cuts because they just don't get enough money from the government. *I* don't want to lose the library, but I don't want the Education Centre to close either and that might be the alternative.'

I sighed. Mum spent more of her evenings at the Education Centre than she did at home these days. The meeting was on Wednesday and I *knew* she wouldn't give up her class to go to it. Still, I'd have to introduce my father, Edward Grey, to the larger-than-life Portland Power, and that was enough contrast for one evening without having to produce Mum in her neat M & S suit as well.

The phone rang. It was Daniella, wanting to know if I was going to the cinema on Sunday. We always went to a film together at the end of a school holiday. I had no real reason to say no, but I hesitated all the same. I'd only known Archie for two days and her family for less than one, but already everything they weren't involved in seemed colourless and uninteresting.

I went to the film. It was the usual kind of hollywood RomCom which I normally found OK, and I ate the usual amount of popcorn and M & Ms, but even Daniella could tell my heart wasn't in it.

'What's up?' she said on the way home.

'They're talking about closing the library,' I said.

'No, really?' said Daniella. She looked quite concerned though I knew it was only because she felt sorry for me. The library didn't mean anything to her. 'Too bad – what'll happen to that bloke you're keen on, Joshua?'

'Joel,' I corrected her miserably. I didn't know. The whole thought of the library not being there, the books being dispersed, Joel and Isis working in other libraries or being made redundant, was more than I could bear to talk about. So I started telling Daniella about Archie. That was a mistake. Daniella's quite possessive. She didn't like the idea that the new girl was already muscling in on 'her' friend she liked it even less that I obviously thought Archie was pretty special.

I could tell she had mentally decided that *she* was going to be the one who decided whether the new girl was worth noticing. In the circumstances I decided not to mention having met the gorgeous Fitzroy and we parted on fairly chilly terms. I had to spend the whole evening in the desert kingdom, just to get myself comfortable again which was no help to my history project on the Bay of Pigs which I was supposed to hand in on Monday.

Dad dropped me off at school on Monday because he had a meeting nearby.

'Just look at that!' he said, pulling up behind the dream van. 'Whatever does it look like? We must have New Age Travellers in the area.' He frowned. 'I don't remember reading about them in the *Advertiser*.'

'It's the Powers' van,' I said swallowing. 'They came all the way from New Zealand in it.' I got out of the car as quickly as I could. 'Bye, Dad. Thanks!'

'Hey, Emily,' Daniella said crossly, as she came over. 'You might have told me you were getting a lift. I waited for you on the corner.'

'Hi, Emma Leigh,' said a Byronic sixth former, unfolding his long legs from the front of Portland's van. 'Hang on, wait for us.'

Daniella stood open-mouthed, as the gorgeous Fitz lounged over and gave me the benefit of his dazzling smile, followed by Archie, managing to look glamorous even in an Elm Park blazer.

'Why didn't you *say*?' Daniella hissed and I knew she wasn't going to be talking to me for the rest of the day.

'See ya,' said Fitz, peeling off towards the sixth form centre, while the rest of us went into the main building.

Archie was put in my set for English and I felt a momentary pang as Mrs Everett greeted her. Eleanor Everett was my favourite teacher and was my class tutor as well as Head of English. She had an acid tongue and was reputed to drink spritzers in the pub with those Upper sixes who were part of her clique. These were the ones who directed the sixth form play which mocked the staff, wrote incomprehensible pieces for the school magazine and wore the most interesting clothes. They were, of course, the group that I aspired to belong to. Mrs Everett wasn't too popular with the Head, but her fans said it was because she never accepted an invitation to drink in the pub with him. Her husband, whom no-one had ever seen, was supposed to be enormously rich and she always wore elegant and expensive clothes.

I was really looking forward to doing A-level English and drinking in the pub with 'Eleanor'. There were signs that she saw me as a potential clique material too. Her comments on my essays were always encouraging and she never said catty things to me. Daniella hated her, though she wasn't in her group for English. I just *knew* Archie was going to be Eleanor's type. We were studying *Macbeth* and she got Archie to read Lady Macbeth. The scene was the one where Macbeth (a.k.a Ryan Duffy) comes in after murdering Duncan. The pair of them were brilliant and I could see Ryan was already smitten with Archie.

If I hadn't already been completely bewitched by Archie, I would have hated her. Pretty, clever, nice, with a really fabulous family and now being given the doggy brown eyes treatment by Ryan, the only halfway decent-looking bloke in my class. And clearly being groomed by Eleanor for the sixth form spritzer set. Oh Archie, hearts were going to break.

'Well done,' said Eleanor briefly. 'Emily, you read the porter speech and give it your usual welly. We're really getting somewhere with this play.'

Immediately I felt included again, and was rewarded at the end of the lesson with both Eleanor's and Archie's approval. At lunch time Daniella turned her back on me with a pointed sort of sniff. I smiled a bit because Dani is hopeless at feuds and sulks; she's much too inquisitive and we both knew I was her best route to Fitz. I'd seen the way she'd ogled him outside the gates.

On our way into afternoon school, Archie pointed at the notice-board. There was another red-for-danger notice about the library and a stack of leaflets on the table underneath.

'Isis has been busy,' she said. '*Or Joel*,' I though, wondering if I'd missed him coming into school. Eleanor was picking up a leaflet.

'Philistines!' she muttered under her breath. It made me smile because she was so unlike Portland the Norseman as she stood there in her pastel Nicole Farhi two-piece, yet I saw them as part of the same team. 'On the side of the angels' that was it. I wished I could see my dad as an angel.

'Have you seen this, girls?' Eleanor demanded.

'Yes,' I nodded.

'My grandmother's going to chair the meeting,' said Archie.

Mrs Everett and I both stared at her.

33

'I forgot to tell you, Archie said, turning to me. 'When we showed her the leaflet, she phoned Isis and offered her services.' Archie looked at Eleanor. 'She's Henrietta Power.' She said it so simply, as if the elegant Eleanor would be sure to have heard of her.

'I would have gone anyway,' said Eleanor, 'but now I know Henrietta Power will be chairing it, wild horses wouldn't keep me away.' I wondered if she really knew who Henrietta was or was just bluffing. Eleanor wasn't the type to admit she didn't know a writer's work. She flashed one of her most charismatic smiles at Archie and disappeared into the staffroom, high heels clicking. She was so beautifully politically incorrect always.

'*My* grandmother's a retired teacher,' I said.

'That's all right,' said Archie. 'Mrs Everett's a teacher!' and we both giggled.

On Wednesday night, after our macaroni cheese supper had been cleared away, I persuaded Dad to walk to the library instead of taking the car.

'It's more ecologically sound,' I said, 'and it's a lovely evening.'

It was. It had been the warmest, most golden autumn I could remember, though the evenings were beginning to get chilly and there was a lovely premonition of real November weather in the mists around the streetlights. There was no sign of the dream van and I had a hunch that Archie had persuaded her family to walk too. I didn't want them to see our dull car and she didn't want anyone to see their interesting one. I was definitely getting the feeling that Archie found her family too conspicuous.

So, when I heard Lisle's deep musical voice whispering 'don't do anything to attract attention to us,' at first I thought it was just my imagination. But then I saw they were all there. Tall Portland, wearing an astonishing green velvet opera cloak, Lisle in her glowing, flowing ethnic garb, Henrietta looking distinguished in some vaguely designer trouser-suit, Fitz looking just too handsome to be walking round in the real world, and Archie, strikingly pretty out of school uniform. They were standing in the foyer of the library with the artistic uncle twins, dressed identically in jeans and big sloppy sweaters. The Powers made a formidable group and I had to smile at the idea that they weren't to make too big an impression on people. They had already attracted a crowd.

'Is that a group of actors?' asked Dad and I braced myself for the introductions. Actually it went very well.

'An accountant?' said Henrietta. 'How marvellous! I might need some help sorting out my tax while we're over here.'

Dad was flattered. He hadn't heard of her but he liked the idea of working for an author and she was the least outlandish-looking of this extraordinary family. He gave her his card and we all trooped upstairs to the meeting room. There was an impressive turn out of local supporters.

Isis called the meeting to order and introduced Henrietta as 'the best-selling New Zealand novelist' and Joel said a bit about the council's plans to close the library to save money and then the meeting was thrown open to anyone to say anything. A very angry young man from the local Socialist Workers' Party was demanding a sit-in and everyone was looking at him. I was just thinking that he looked a bit like the rat-faced traitor I had thrown to the crocodiles in the imperial salt-lake the previous week, when I suddenly noticed Fitzroy out of the corner of my eye. Or rather I noticed that he wasn't there. He had been standing near the back door.

I don't really know why I was looking that direction except that I was sort of hoping that Mrs Everett would show up soon. Fitz had been leaning against a pillar, in the same position as that Elizabethan courtier, you know the one in the famous picture, with a lacy collar and a flower in his hand, leaning up against a tree. Well, one second Fitz was there and the next he wasn't. I blinked and then he was back, only he was leaning against the other side of the pillar. He looked like a mirror-image of the way he had bee before. He caught my eye and looked uncomfortable. It was too late. He had 'drawn attention' to himself – and the attention was mine.

3

A new dimension

After that I found it very difficult to concentrate on the meeting. There was a heated discussion about what the new organisation to save the library should be called. The older people at the meeting wanted 'Friends of Oak Grove' (Fogies – just the wrong image); the younger ones, like the socialist worker, favoured 'Oak Grove Action Group'. The young ones won, because Henrietta suggested the modification: 'Action Group for Oak Grove' which spelt out 'AGOG!' Everyone liked that, even though it didn't really mean much. It sounded alert and active.

'Trust a writer,' said Dad, as we walked home, but he said it as if he approved, not in his usual sarcastic way about anyone different from him. I should have been pleased but now I had my own worries about Archie's family. What had happened to Fitz? There was no logical explanation; he had simply vanished and reappeared. In a way, I was used to this kind of thing. It happened in the desert kingdom all the time. You can't really mix with sorcerers and witch-kings and not expect all kinds of shape-shifting, clairvoyance, telekinesis and other manifestations of natural and unnatural magic. But it was a shock to come up against it in Lark Hill Forest.

Even seeing Eleanor Everett arrive with a man in an exquisitely cut overcoat couldn't distract me from Fitz's disappearing act. Should I challenge Archie about it or not? Whatever kind of magician or alien her brother was, the whole family was the same. I remembered the little tingle I'd felt when I'd first met the grown-ups and Lisle saying 'Don't draw attention to us'. There was some sort of secret about them and I was scared to find out what it was.

I decided to concentrate on the library campaign. Henrietta had formed an AGOG! Committee and I was 'student representative'. It sounded good but I had no idea what I was supposed to do. Amazingly, my Dad had volunteered to be the treasurer. There was no money yet, but we were going to charge £2 a year to join (50p for children, students, OAPs and UB40s). People were encouragingly angry about the plans to close the library. Even quite ordinary people, who had never protested about anything before, were going to write letters to councillors, take round petitions and join demonstrations outside the Town Hall.

Mrs Everett was going to take charge of press and

publicity and Henrietta said, if the campaign was going to take a long time, she would write a regular newsletter for members. As for me, I was ready to do anything that would save my beloved library, *particularly* if it meant working alongside all my favourite people. Joel and Isis weren't supposed to campaign at all; as employees of the council, they were meant to keep apart from anything remotely political. But that didn't stop them attending AGOG! committee meetings.

The first one was at the Powers' house on the Friday after the big protest meeting. Mum gave Dad and me an odd look as we set off. It was one of the rare nights she didn't have an evening class, so perhaps she'd have liked to spend it with us. But I don't think she really minded, as she was already getting out her books and preparing to write an essay. Can you enter the mind of a grown-up actually *volunteering* to do homework? My homework was already suffering, as a result of all the time I was giving to the library but Dad surprised me by saying I could catch up at the weekend. It made me feel a bit guilty about all the hours I'd spent reading fantasy books from Oak Grove, although I *did* use it for homework research too. But, if I'm honest, it wouldn't be computers and databases I'd miss if the library closed down, it would be fuel for the desert kingdom. And Joel.

Fitz opened the door in Avenue Road and I saw a flicker of anxiety cross his dark romantic features when he saw it was me.

'Good evening, young man,' said my father, his personality equivalent of a room-freshener dispelling all feelings of danger and excitement. 'We've come for the library meeting.'

Fitzroy showed us into the big living room, which was already looking quite different from the last time I'd seen it. Al the packing cases had gone. The furniture was quite old and shabby but Lisle – I was sure it must have been Lisle – had draped chairs and sofas with brightly patterned throws. Dried sunflowers glowed in the grate and the room was softly lit with coloured lamps and some floating candles in big blue glass bowls filled with those shiny rainbow nuggets. I could feel Dad's eyebrows raise behind me and I'm sure he was thinking that it would be a difficult room to do a crossword in.

Eleanor Everett was on a chaise-longue talking to Archie, her pale designer clothes looking a bit washed out against the vibrant colours of Lisle's living-room. Joel and Isis were already there, sitting on large mirror-work floor cushions. Dad sat down on the edge of an extravagantly comfortable armchair draped in peacock-patterned cloth and I sat between Archie and Mrs Everett on a velvet floor cushion very like the one my tame panther lay on in the desert kingdom.

Have you noticed how boring adults can be when they get together to talk about something? Quite a lot of them seemed to be more interested in listening to the sound of their own voices than in saving the library. But Joel and Isis seemed happy enough; I think they were just relieved that someone was doing something.

I drifted off to the desert kingdom.

Krin was cold, cold with that bitter chill that comes in on the desert wind when night falls. K'sedra was pacing wearily through her state rooms, her long velvet dress swishing on the marble floors. Her black panther, Mirza, padded softly along beside her, turning with her as her restless steps took her back and forth. Suddenly she stopped and caressed the beast's silky ears.

'Oh, Mirza, what am I to do?' she whispered, gazing into his yellow eyes. 'There is treachery afoot in Krin. Who can be trusted? One of my court is in the pay of Prince Khalid, I'm sure. Khalid knows my every move before I make it. He may even be spying on me himself, since he has the gift of invisibility. A dangerous game but not beyond the audacity of that brigand. I am so alone, Mirza. You are the only one who serves me faithfully and truly.' She rubbed her face along the top of the great cat's head.

Someone speaking my name jerked me back to the here and now.

'Emma Leigh,' said Henrietta, with that little hiatus between the second and third syllables and stress on the last that turned me into such a different person. 'Have you any ideas about how we can get young people involved in the campaign?'

'I'm sure they'll come on a demo,' I said instantly, looking up at Mrs Everett, who nodded her agreement. 'And probably on a sit-in too, if it comes to it. They'd be better at that sort of thing that writing to councillors.'

'Good,' said Henrietta. 'That'll make good photographs for the newspapers and on TV – young people waving banners about the library.'

'I could help Emma with those,' volunteered Archie. 'What should the banners say?'

We agreed to hold a demonstration outside the town hall in two weeks' time. Now came the fun part of the meeting.

'The pen is mightier than the axe', was one slogan. 'Don't cut down Oak Grove' was another obvious one but as the evening wore on, they got more militant and daring, criticising the councillors directly, particularly Councillor Bliss, Chair of the Leisure Services Committee. 'Councillors who close libraries should be shelved' and 'Ignorance is Bliss' were the most popular. Everyone left feeling quite hopeful and exhilarated.

There was no chance to talk alone to Archie but she kept giving me sideways looks. We hadn't really spent much time together over the last two days; not that she was avoiding me, but I had the uncomfortable feeling that Fitz had told her about what I'd seen him do at the meeting. I didn't know whether to say anything to her about it or not. Part of me was beginning to wonder whether I'd imagined the whole thing and endowed Fitz with some of Khalid's powers, but who was I trying to kid? I *knew* I had seen him vanish and reappear.

On Saturday morning I couldn't stand it any longer. I phoned Archie and, taking the future of our friendship in both hands, said; 'Look, I know there's something strange about your family.'

'Oh,' came her disembodied voice over the phone. Not being able to see her made it easier.

'Fitzroy disappeared at that meeting, didn't he?' I gabbled. 'Don't try to pretend he didn't. I saw him. You're not really from New Zealand at all, are you?'

44

There was such a long silence that I thought she was going to hang up on me, then her voice returned, much louder and clearer. 'No, we're not from New Zealand. We're from another dimension.'

I turned, the phone still in my hand. The reason Archie's voice was so much easier to hear was that she was standing in my room.

'Trust you to be different,' I said, and then I fainted.

When I came round, I found that Archie had switched off my phone and was sitting on my bed calmly waiting for me to pull myself together. She didn't volunteer anything else beyond her original statement. But I couldn't just ignore that fact that one minute Archie had been at the house in Avenue Road and the next in my bedroom. Crass or not, I was going to mention it.

'How did you do that?' I asked.

'It's called teleporting,' said Archie. 'It's what I do. You can get from one place to another without using the topography of a single dimension.'

'Oh,' I said. 'I see.' (I didn't.) 'Was that what Fitz did?' It seemed incredibly pointless to use such a terrific skill as teleporting to move from one side of a pillar to the other. Archie hesitated. I could tell she didn't really want to tell me any more than she had to.

'No,' she said, at last. 'He's a time-traveller. He just moved into the future an hour or two and misjudged his return.'

It had the form of an explanation without the content.

I think I adjusted brilliantly to having a friend from another dimension. Some might say it was because I didn't spend that much time in this one anyway. I definitely felt a bit spooked and, though I hate to admit it, a bit upstaged by the whole Power family. But if you're thinking Archie and I sat down together for a long girlish chat together about parallel universes and hyperspace, you couldn't be more wrong. Everything I found out then about her family and everything I've found out since, over several months, I've had to drag out and piece together. It was as if they had a guilty secret, a skeleton in the family cupboard, that it just wouldn't be good taste to mention. It's far the best way, of course, for stopping people talking about something. I wouldn't want Eleanor Everett to know I had a poster of Pete Doherty on my bedroom wall or that I really enjoyed Tolkien.

But for now I was prepared to be tasteless.

'Why?' I asked. 'Why did he go to the future?'

'He wanted to check whether the meeting was

going to get rough. He didn't like the way that socialist worker was talking. You remember he said people couldn't expect to guarantee that there wouldn't be any violence? Well, Fitz thought he'd check that nothing was going to break out that evening. It was very stupid of him.'

'Why? Because he couldn't do anything about it?'

'No. He could have placed a 999 call about five minutes before any fighting started. What was stupid was drawing attention to himself in a public place. After all, if *you* noticed, *anyone* could have.'

'Thanks,' I said.

'You know what I mean,' said Archie. 'My parents were furious with him and he's strictly grounded now.'

I couldn't help it. The idea of 'grounding' someone who could flit between different points in time was irresistibly funny. I started to smile. Archie caught my eye and relaxed.

'He's very peeved about it,' she said, smiling too. 'He's doing History A-level you see and he thought he'd have it dead cushy with his assignments.'

By now we were both laughing and things didn't seem so bad. It could be really good fun knowing people form another dimension.

'Can you all do something?' I asked, though I could guess the answer.

'Ye-es,' said Archie, still reluctant to give anything away.

'Well, come on then,' I bullied. 'Tell me what I've let myself in for.'

'It's difficult,' said Archie slowly. 'You see, where we come from everything is very different from here. *We* are very different when we are there. What you call 'doing something', by which you mean something not possible in this dimension, is commonplace there. We can *all* do things like teleporting, time-travelling, shape-shifting, and so on, because we aren't bound by the same physical laws as this universe.'

A cold feeling crept down the back of my sweatshirt.

'You don't even *look* human, do you?' I asked.

'No,' said Archie, looking very uncomfortable. 'We have assumed acceptable forms for our time in this dimension.'

'What would you look like there?' I asked, not sure I wanted to know.

'You don't want to know,' said Archie. 'It would only upset you.' She was right. I was thinking of that old film I saw on TV where a man looks through a keyhole at a woman taking off her clothes and then she takes off *her body* and is a glowing yellow alien underneath.

'Well, what dimension is it then? I mean which. Fifth? Seventh?'

'Does it matter?'

It didn't of course. It wasn't as if I'd met anyone from the sixth or eighth and was trying to see where the Powers fitted in my collection. Then I thought of something else.

'You said you call all time-travel where you came from. But just now you said Fitz was a time-traveller, as if that was his special thing.'

Archie frowned. 'We don't quite understand ourselves how it works, but here it seems as if our skills have been shared out across the group, as if each of us can only do one thing. Mine is teleporting. Fitz's is time-travelling. But we haven't worked out exactly what each of us can do. And it's too dangerous to experiment. We don't want to draw attention to ourselves.'

I was thinking furiously. She had said 'the group' as if she were talking about the company of actors my father had mistaken them for.

'You're not even really a family, are you?'

'That is a concept of your dimension,' said Archie stiffly. 'It is convenient for us to assume the forms of a human family so that we can keep together. We don't have families where we come from.'

'Too grand?' I said. All this 'my dimension, your dimension' stuff was beginning to get on my nerves. I couldn't help living in my own universe and though I was quite willing to believe that the Powers came from a superior one, I didn't like having it rubbed in.

'You wanted a special friend, didn't you?' asked Archie.

'Yes I did, but if you're so concerned about not being noticed – and you've mentioned it several times – you would have done better to imitate a family like mine.'

Again that sideways shift of the eyes. There was something she wasn't telling me. I decided to let it rest for now.

'Anyway, why is it so important not to be noticed?'

'Well, for a start, we don't want people to know that we are – well – not like others. They would write about us in your tabloids and we would be hounded by paparazzi and journalists with cheque-books.'

'I see you've done your research,' I said dryly. 'But that's not all it is, is it? I mean, why did you come here in the first place?'

Archie looked as if she was calculating exactly how much it was safe to tell me. Mind you, she had looked like that ever since she had arrived in my bedroom.

'We had to move to another dimension,' she said at

last, 'at least temporarily. I don't know how to explain it to you. Everything is so different here. But in the terms of your world, I suppose you could say we were being persecuted by other beings. We had to escape.'

'And they don't know where you are?' Light was beginning to dawn.

'That's right,' said Archie. 'A lot of what we appear to do here involves slipping briefly into other dimensions. Let me see if I can show you.' At first I thought she was going to fly across the room but she just walked in a perfectly ordinary way over to my desk.

'Can I use this paper and scissors?'

'Of course,' I said, fascinated. She sat at my white desk cutting something out, looking like any other teenager. Yet what was she? What did she look like where the Powers had come from? Would I even recognise her or would she just be a swirl of coloured energy?

She held up a paper man, like the ones you make strings of in nursery school:

'You see this man?'

'Yeah, he looks a bit like Ryan Duffy.'

'OK, let's call him Ryan,' agreed Archie. 'Come over here.'

She put Ryan down on a clean sheet of paper and drew a box round him.

'I've put him in prison,' she said.

'Why, what did he do?'

'Nothing. He's a two-dimensional man, so I can imprison him for ever by putting him in a two-dimensional box. He can't get out however he tries.'

I felt sorry for Ryan. He looked so helpless spread out there on my A4 homework pad, a bit like one of those poor pinned butterflies you see in museums.

'But *I* can easily get him out,' said Archie, picking up the flat little man, 'by moving him into another dimension here.' She let the paper man dangle from her fingers. 'Think how that seems to him! Ryan simply can't understand the physical laws of a dimension he's never been in. And think how it would seem to his two-dimensional jailers on the outside of the box. They'd think Ryan had simply vanished.'

'Just like Fitz,' I said.

Archie nodded. 'Of course, that's not a completely accurate demonstration,' she said, dropping the fluttering Ryan in my wastepaper-basket, 'because the cut-out Ryan does have three dimensions – he's just very flat. You must imagine I lifted him off the page I drew him on.'

My head was already spinning but it was going to get worse.

'When you cross dimensions like that it sends ripples through all of them,' Archie continued. 'My … parents are concerned that every time one of us does something that isn't possible in this dimension we might be sending signals that will allow our enemies to track us down. That's why they were so angry with Fitz.'

I thought a bit. 'But doesn't that mean you've sent out some more of those signals by teleporting over here?' I said.

Archie frowned. 'It was a risk we had to take. I had to convince you about what we are. Would you have believed me if I'd just told you over the phone?'

I didn't know. No one had ever told me before that they came from another dimension. I certainly wouldn't have believed it of Daniella, or my Mum, not even of someone really exciting and lovely like Isis. Archie took my silence for agreement. She slid off my chair. 'But I shan't risk it going back. I shall walk from here to there like the ordinary human being I'm supposed to be.'

'We're not *that* ordinary you know,' I said, feeling less than enchanted with Archie for the first time in our short friendship. 'I mean, I know *I* am and so are my family, but Shakespeare was a human being too and what about Leonardo da Vinci and Stephen Hawking ...'

Archie stepped closer. 'Don't let's quarrel about it,' she said. 'And I don't think you're at all ordinary. In fact you're much more special than you realise.'

She flashed me one of her million-gigawatts-worth-of-charisma smiles and left the room. When she had gone, I fished Ryan out of my wastepaper-basket and stuck him on my notice-board with a bit of blue-tack. I couldn't bear to put a drawing pin through him. I knew just how he felt.

4

Demonstrative

It wasn't long before I saw Archie again because we were on AGOG! recruitment duty in the library that afternoon. It was brilliant. The Powers had made a big notice-board which was propped up against the wall beside the counter. We had a table in front of it, with a pile of leaflets and membership forms designed on a computer and photocopied by Mrs Everett and a proper cash-box supplied by my father to put the subs in. We were kept pretty busy, as people were attracted by the SAVE OUR LIBRARY sign in huge red letters on the notice-board.

Joel was on duty that afternoon and brought us cups of tea in a slack moment (one of his, not ours). He couldn't carry a book *and* two cups so he seemed sort of more there than usual. He really looked at me and gave me a proper smile. But if I'm honest, I have to admit he looked longer at Archie. I felt that pang that comes from having a friend you like a lot who's prettier than you. But there was no doubt that Joel knew who

I was now and was grateful for my help.

Mrs Everett dropped in to see how we were getting on. It made me smile that she was wearing one of her more vividly coloured outfits and a brilliant red lipstick. So she was suffering from Power-contrast too! She had brought more supplies of leaflets and we needed them too. We had so many new members we were running out.

'Do you want any help mobilising the Elm Park students?' Mrs Everett asked me.

'Yes, that'd be great,' I said.

'Why don't you both meet me outside the staffroom at morning break on Monday?' she volunteered. This was almost as good as being part of the spritzer set.

Our next visitor was Daniella. I didn't think she'd ever *been* in Oak Grove library before. She took a book out though. Had the nerve to ask Joel to recommend something romantic. (She got more than she bargained for though because he gave her *Dr Zhivago*. Maybe she thought it was one of those hospital soaps about nurses having affairs with consultants.) She wandered over with her large slab of book under her arm and casually asked if she could join the group.

'That'll be fifty pence to you,' I said briskly, giving her a membership form.

'What's this about a demo?' she said, filling in her name.

'It's in two weeks' time,' said Archie. 'All the details are on this leaflet.'

'And we'll probably have a meeting in school about it some time next week,' I added.

'Your family going on it?' she asked, looking vaguely somewhere between us. I had to smile.

'I might get my dad to come,' I said.

'Yes, I think all mine will,' said Archie.

There was no time to say more but I could see Daniella was satisfied. It was worth fifty pence to get close to the gorgeous Fitz. I wondered what she'd think if she knew he was a time-traveller from somewhere in hyperspace. She'd probably just shrug and say 'nobody's perfect'.

Ryan Duffy dropped by too and Archie and I exchanged guilty looks. He seemed so sturdily three-dimensional.

'Hi, Emily,' he said. We had been in the same class for three years and this was only about the third time he had spoken to me. But Archie was dealing with another person. Ryan coughed up his fifty pence and showed as much enthusiasm for the march as Daniella. It was beginning to seem as if we'd get a lot of support from

people who fancied various members of the Power family.
I wondered if we should put some pin-up photos of them
on the notice-board with captions: 'Use Oak Grove and
you can look like this'.

'I didn't know you were into books, Ryan,'
I said nastily.

'You know me, Emily,' he said. 'Literature, poetry,
Shakespeare – can't get enough of it. In fact, I think I'll
take something out now.' He sloped off to the teenage
section and took out a Darren Shan. At least, he tried. I've
got very good hearing and, even though I was enrolling
another AGOG! member at the time, I could still hear Joel
politely telling Ryan he'd need to have a library card if he
wanted to take a book home. I bent my head diligently
over the membership forms so he wouldn't know I'd
rumbled him.

By five o'clock closing time, we had recruited forty
members and the people on morning duty had got fifty-
five. So, with the committee, we had over a hundred
members and about £150 in the cash box. Archie and I
walked to the corner where our routes home branched.

'It was good, wasn't it?' she said.

'Yeah, excellent,' I said. 'But I don't understand why
your family are doing all this. Why *do* you care about the
library? I mean, why would you care about books and

reading and stuff like that when you don't even come from here?'

'It's a very special place to us,' she said, lowering her voice and looking round to make sure no one was listening. 'I can't tell you why now, but I will some other time if I can. Meanwhile, it's enough that it's important to you and people like you.'

I must have looked as dumb as I felt. 'You're fighting to save the library because of me?' I asked.

'Partly,' said Archie, pushing back a chestnut curl that the wind had blown across her face. 'But I can't talk about it now. Portland's coming to meet me.'

I noticed she had given up words like 'father' since she'd admitted the Powers were just a bunch of superheroes. I thought I could see his massive frame looming in the distance through the early November mists, so I let her go. She'd tell me more if she could, I knew. I set off down the road, clutching the membership forms and the cash-box. I wished I'd brought my rucksack or at least a plastic bag to disguise the box. I began to feel nervous. The box seemed to grow larger and heavier in my hands as I walked along and it made obvious clinking money noises, even though I tried to hold it steady. And as the box grew larger in my mind, so I felt smaller and more vulnerable. A group of young men emerged out of the mists. I tried to hide the box under my jacket. Have you ever tried to hide a large metal cash-box under your denim jacket? It doesn't work. As the group came closer, laughing and punching one another's shoulders, I got more scared. I always feel like that about people bigger and taller than me, even when they're not threatening at all. They seem like Alsatian dogs, nine times out of ten friendly and safe. But it's the tenth time I'm always dreading, the sudden lunge, the snapping white teeth.

'Hi, titch,' said on of the men. 'What you got there?' and I knew it was the tenth time. I closed my eyes and saw myself in the palace grounds of my home in the desert kingdom.

> Intruders had climbed over the wall, somehow evading the palace guards. They dared to surround the sacred body of the Empress-Mage. She drew herself up to her full imposing height and cried 'Mirza!'. Her black panther bounded growling out of the night and hurled himself at the ringleader.

'Aaargh!'

The blood-curdling cry was so near and so real that I opened my eyes. There was growling somewhere. The louts were scattering, running away as fast as they could.

A sleek, black, muscular beast was in full pursuit. It disappeared into the mists after them. I was trembling with fright but still clutching the cash-box. Archie stood beside me, her arm round my shoulders.

'What was that?' I stammered.

'That was Portland,' said Archie. She sounded almost as surprised as me. 'I guess that means he's the shape-shifter.'

A growling noise came out of the mist and I shivered some more. But the figure that emerged was two-legged – Portland in his usual form, huge and bearded and rumbling his disapproval of thugs who would menace a young girl.

'You shouldn't have been allowed to carry money home on your own,' he said. 'Archie and I will escort you the rest of the way.'

'What did you do to them?' I asked, half-dreading the answer.

'Just gave them a good scare,' said Portland, showing his white teeth. 'I don't think they'll try that again in a hurry.'

Archie started to laugh. 'Portland, you're such an idiot.'

'Why?' he said, offended.

'Did you really think you had to *change* to scare

those boys?' she asked.

I saw the joke and started to laugh too. Portland himself was quite enough to terrify most people on a dark night. I suddenly felt very glad that he was on my side. Portland smiled. 'I didn't seem to have much choice about it,' he said. 'A black panther was definitely being summoned and as the nearest shape-shifter available, I had to oblige.'

I stopped laughing abruptly. 'You mean, *I* did that?'

'You do more than you realise, Emma Leigh,' said Archie softly. 'But seriously Portland, although we know what it is you can do here now, was it wise to do it? Won't there be ... consequences?'

'You're a fine one to talk,' said Portland. 'Who teleported us to the spot where Emma was in trouble? And that's the second time you've done it today. Who *exactly* is risking 'consequences' here?'

They stopped and glared at each other. They had completely given up playing father and daughter in front of me. It was obvious that Portland knew that I had discovered what he and Archie were and they could drop their guard. Whatever they had been where they came from (wherever *that* was) it was clear they were equals and used to arguing on equal terms. Come to think of it, there had been an element of that even when they were playing happy families in the supermarket. It was one of the things I found attractive about the Powers, that the children were listened to and had a say in what went on. I sighed. Perhaps you had to be from another dimension before your parents treated you like another human being – or another coloured swirl of energy, as the case might be. But just at the moment all I wanted was to get home to my perfectly ordinary parents and curl up in an armchair with a cup of hot chocolate and a good book.

'Look,' I said. 'Can you argue about this later? It really hasn't anything to do with me and I'm feeling a bit peculiar.'

They were immediately all concern. But I didn't miss the split second glance they exchanged when I said it didn't have anything to do with me. Portland gently removed the cash-box from my numb fingers and Archie took the rather crushed membership forms. They each put an arm round me and frogmarched me home.

'Don't tell Dad about those men,' I whispered as I rang the doorbell. But I needn't have worried. Portland handed the cash-box reverently to my father as if he'd carried it every step of the way from the library. They didn't stay to chat, even though Dad did politely invite them in. I collapsed into a chair.

'I'm absolutely pooped,' I said.

'What an unfortunate expression, Emily,' said my father. 'But you do look tired. Would you like some hot chocolate?'

At that moment I didn't want to change dear old predictable Edward Grey for dangerous, exciting Portland Power at all.

On the day of the demo I was glad to be marching in the midst of a glamorous group of Powers. It was the most mixed collection of demonstrators that Lark Hill Forest had ever seen (not that it had seen many). The marchers assembled in Oak Grove library in the early evening and the numbers were pretty impressive even if the people themselves were individually less than alarming.

I looked with satisfaction at the Elm Park contingent. Not just Ryan and Daniella and lots of other Year 10s but lots of Year 11s and sixth-formers too, all carrying placards and banners. Ever since I'd been at Elm Park I'd tried to do things like getting a part in the school play and found myself outstripped by the older students. I'd been an attendant and a lady-in-waiting but never had a speaking part. And now all these glamorous fifth and sixth-formers were here because of me! Even Gabrielle Connell, who had played Juliet, Viola, and Maria in *West Side Story*, in our school productions and already been accepted by RADA. The photographer for the local paper had homed in on Gabrielle like an Exocet and was already clicking his camera in her lovely actorish face.

As we milled around, lots of the older students checked in with me about details of the demo; even Jacob Morse (otherwise known as Romeo, Orsino and Tony) came and asked me if his placard was OK. Suddenly everyone knew who I was. It wasn't the same as being popular but it was a lot better than being anonymous. I was quite busy handing out 'Save Our Library' sashes and AGOG! badges to supporters. We even had fourteen Year 7s who were supposed to display the letters of 'Save Our Library' and they were particularly difficult to keep in the right order. When we were ready to move off, the signal was given by Portland who had a totally unnecessary megaphone and I took my place near the head of the march between Archie and Fitz.

In front, the twin Power uncles, perfectly matched in height, were at either end of a big banner, followed by Henrietta, Portland and Lisle, all carrying placards. Behind us were the rest of the Elm Park students, with Mrs Everett. She wouldn't carry a banner but had agreed to wear a sash, since the green complemented her smart red coat. Dad was helping to marshall the large contingent of middle-aged and elderly supporters, mostly women in woolly hats. Joel and Isis brought up the rear with all the twenty-somethings pushing toddlers in buggies or carrying babies in slings. The *Advertiser* photographer liked them almost as much as he liked Gabrielle.

Marching along between Fitz and Archie, I felt a real rush of pride. It wasn't just that they were so beautiful and striking and were my friends. I felt proud of *all* the Lark Hill Foresters: the woolly-hatted grannies, the Elm Park teenagers, the sticky toddlers and all. Even if people had come for all kinds of mixed motives, they were all proclaiming that the library mattered to them. Because I only ever used it after school, all sorts of people that I'd never seen in the library turned out to be supporters – the Asian woman from the Post Office, the man from the greengrocers and several waiters from the Chinese restaurant (had they closed for the evening?).

As we got nearer to the Town Hall, several hangers-on joined in, just for the fun. There were some young homeless people, who rolled up their sleeping bags and tagged along with their dogs. As we passed the Red Lion, one or two drunks who had probably been refused any more drinks, wavered uncertainly along the column, breathing beer fumes over Eleanor, Archie, Gabrielle and any other attractive female within their reach. Few stayed the course all the way to the Town Hall.

When we got there we joined up with several other marchers waving placards and chanting various badly-rehearsed slogans. They had set off from the swimming pool, the nursery and the Youth Club, all threatened by the cuts. Everything got a bit mixed up at that stage. Lots of the Elm Park sixth-formers wandered off to mingle with the Youth Club supporters and swimming pool demonstrators, while the buggy brigade merged with the nursery school protestors. That was OK, really. I felt a bit bad about doing so much for the library when all the other causes were so worthy too, but I'd long outgrown the nursery, was too young for the Youth club and couldn't swim, so it had to be the library for me.

The councillors were arriving for the meeting and we had great fun spotting them and rushing forward with leaflets as they tried to slink in unnoticed. Mrs Everett was particularly brilliant at recognising them and commandeered the photographer, pointing him at embarrassed councillors having handfuls of leaflets thrust in their faces. Every time we caught one, all the demonstrators surged forward, brandishing their placards and chanting. I kept the seventh years conspicuous at the front and roughly in the right order (at one point they had spelt YOUR LIBRA SAVER). I *think* they were sending the right message when their photographs were taken. I caught my father's eye across the mob. He was looking flushed and excited and not at all his usual calm self. This whole business was stirring up people who were normally law-abiding citizens. Not that we were breaking any laws. Dad had checked out the rules of public assembly straight after the first meeting.

All of a sudden there was a bigger rush than before and a chant went up of 'BLISS, BLISS, BLISS, OUT, OUT, OUT!' I looked round and saw it was being orchestrated by Dave, the Socialist Worker. I was annoyed about it because I thought we shouldn't turn the councillor who held Oak Grove's fate in his hands into an enemy. I pushed through the crowd and tried to get a glimpse of the infamous library-closer.

He looked perfectly ordinary, a smallish, bald man in a big coat, quite bewildered by all the noise and shouting. Lisle was talking to him quietly and giving him an AGOG! leaflet. He took it automatically with the other pieces of paper pushed at him by demonstrators.

'Thank you, thank you,' he said politely. 'Er, good evening.' And he ducked into the Town Hall entrance. After that there wasn't much more we could do. We weren't allowed to take placards into the meeting and there were far too many of us for the public gallery. If we'd known about it earlier we could have organised a delegation but we were saving that for the next meeting, when we were going to present our petition. It seemed that no final decision about the cuts was going to be made until just before Christmas. It was all a bit of an anti-climax really. There was nothing to do but find our banners and shuffle off.

It would have been so different in Krin. I could imagine what Khalid would have made of a demonstration outside his palace. At a single word from him, a cohort of brawny soldiers with gleaming scimitars would have dispersed the mob, or a least bits of it.

But I cheered up when all the committee plus Joel and Isis went back for coffee and a post mortem at the Powerhouse, as people had started calling it. I volunteered to help Lisle and the uncles in the kitchen. As she spooned ground coffee into two large brass cafetieres and we loaded trays with mugs and cups, I asked:

'Couldn't you do something different to save the library?'

'I think the demonstration went very well,' said Lisle, lifting her branching eyebrows. 'What would you have?'

'I don't know,' I said. 'But you *could* do anything, couldn't you? Strike Councillor Bliss dead. Put more money into the Council's bank account. Turn the leader of the Council into a frog.'

'We aren't witches, you know,' said Grosvenor.

'Or assassins,' said Albemarle.

'What good would that do?' said Lisle. 'Can't you see the headlines?

LIBRARY SAVED BY EXTRA-TERRESTRIALS
ALIENS LOVE BOOKS.'

'Would it matter, as long as we saved the library?' I argued. I was beginning to feel that the Power family weren't pulling their weight. They'd worked fantastically hard as real people of course, but only I knew how much more weight they were capable of pulling. And none of them had done anything supernatural since Portland's panther impression.

'It's too dangerous,' said Albemarle.

'We might never get back,' said Grosvenor.

'Shhh!' warned Lisle, her eyes snapping at them, but too late.

'We won't get back anyway if they close the library,' said Albemarle.

'Where's the coffee, then?' Portland burst in, rubbing his hand, his ruddy cheeks glowing like a character in a Dickens Christmas story. 'What's the matter? Why are you all glaring at one another?'

You could have cut the atmosphere in that kitchen with a coffee spoon. I was beginning to understand why they cared so much about Oak Grove.

5

Gateways

We had to wait two whole days for the local paper to come out but it was worth it – we made the front page! STUDENTS MARCH FOR LIBRARY! was the banner headline, which was a bit hard on all the other demonstrators. There was a large picture of Gabrielle's tragic expression with her big dark eyes staring out of her photogenic face and her 'Save Our Library' sash clearly visible. There was a smaller, rather fuzzier picture of the letter-holding Year 7s (in the right order, thank goodness) and you could even see half of me, organising them. Mrs Everett pinned the front page story up on the main school notice-board and gave me a discreet thumbs-up during registration. All day older students kept coming up to give me a friendly pat on the back and ask if I'd seen the paper. Gabrielle was the centre of a little group of admirers, but what was new? She was another of those beautiful people who are unfortunately also nice.

You needn't think I waited to tackle Archie about

what I'd heard in the kitchen. But there wasn't much I could do that night as Dad soon marched me home with stern cries of 'Homework!'. By the next day I felt I had to talk to her or burst, so I made her bunk off games. This was stupid, because Archie was good at games (naturally) and noticeable with it. I was hopeless at all games and PE, but, since I'd never missed a lesson before, that would be noticeable too. Still, I couldn't help it. I'd been thinking so continuously about the Powers and their connection with the library, that I'd hardly spent any time in the desert kingdom lately. In fact I couldn't remember the last time I'd been there. Perhaps it was when Portland had turned himself into my black panther, Mirza? There was something funny about that too. He had said 'someone was summoning a black panther'. The more I thought about it, the more everything that had happened so far was connected to me or the library. And I couldn't wait another minute to find out why.

As soon as the bell went for lesson changeover I grabbed Archie and dragged her off to the sixth form centre while everyone else was streaming off to the cloakroom to get changed. Mercifully, there was no one there, which meant we were safe for a double period.

'What is it?' said Archie, half-laughing and half-serious at my sudden transformation into a delinquent.

'We'll get into trouble, you know.'

'What does it matter to you?' I asked. 'This is all a charade anyway, coming to classes, wearing uniform, doing homework. I mean, it's not as if you'll actually be sitting any GCSEs or even be around for French exchange or magazine day or the next school play. You'll be fed up of playing humans long before then and be back to being coloured blobs in Dimension X.' To my utter horror I burst into tears.

Archie didn't like displays of emotion. I knew instinctively that none of the Powers did. It was as if whatever training course they'd put themselves through before coming here just hadn't included feelings and they didn't know how they were supposed to react. So she sat watching uncomfortably while I sobbed, then snuffled and finally whimpered myself to a standstill. Fortunately there was a large box of tissues on one of the coffee tables. After seriously depleting it, I gave a big sigh and felt a bit better.

'It is easier to have an ordinary friend,' Archie stated. 'Daniella doesn't make you cry.'

'No,' I admitted. 'Though I might if I knew she was going away for ever.'

'But we *are* your friends,' she went on, 'even if we don't know how to make you happy.'

'You do make me happy,' I said pathetically. 'It's

been brilliant knowing you and your family, even before I knew you were – you know – different. I mean, you were different enough before, just being you. What I can't bear is knowing one day you'll go the way you came and there'll be nothing I can do about it, any more than I did about your coming. I won't even be able to write to you. You can't have a pen-pal in another dimension.'

That infectious twinkle was back in Archie's eyes. 'It might put a bit of a strain on the postman,' she said.

We were both thinking of arthritic old Bill who delivered letters, very slowly, to both our streets.

'That's better,' said Archie. 'Now you are the old Emma Leigh again. And what made you think you had nothing to do with our coming here? We couldn't have done it without you!'

'What do you mean?' I gaped.

'Has it ever occurred to you,' said Archie, 'that we resemble people from Krin?'

'Well, yes, Fitz is a lot like Prince Khalid. I thought so the first time I saw him ... hey, hang on. What do you know about Krin?'

I had never told her; I had never told *anyone*. It was my secret place, my secret life, where the real me could be found.

'Are you a telepath now as well as a teleporter?'

I demanded.

'We are all telepaths when it comes to the desert kingdom, Emma Leigh.'

This was getting really spooky. I fully expected her eyes to change colour or for her to walk through a wall. The Powers were a kind of walking special effects studio and I never knew what they might do next. But Archie continued to sit on the beige tweed armchair in her navy uniform, just like a real Elm Park student. But not only was she from another dimension – which was surely enough – she now seemed to be claiming to be from a place I had *invented*!

Archie closed her eyes and intoned: 'The desert kingdom of Krin is ringed by the Okona mountains. It is ruled by an Empress-Mage, elected not hereditary. The present ruler K'sedra was chosen like her predecessors at an early age and brought up by priestesses to learn the necessary arts. Her sapphire palace is in an oasis at the heart of the desert. Her palace guard and her personal army server her well, under General Borghul, in the ongoing battles with the many princedoms on the other side of the mountains. Need I go on?'

I felt at once both excited and betrayed. It is not a pleasant experience having your mind invaded. And yet something marvellous was happening too. Perhaps Archie

76

could enter the desert kingdom with me? I'd never really wanted to share it with anyone before but there had never been anyone like Archway Power to share it with before. One thing was certain. She wasn't sending it up, the way Daniella would have done if she'd ever found out about it. Archie was taking it deadly seriously.

I remembered why I'd made her bunk off games.

'Archie, why is the library so important to you? I've got to know. One of your uncles said something about not getting back.'

'He shouldn't have said that,' said Archie instantly. 'Lisle was very cross with him.'

'But it's true, isn't it?' I insisted. 'There's something about the library that means you *have* to keep it open and I don't think it's just so you can borrow Robin Hobb novels.'

Archie was making one of those small mental calculations that always showed so clearly in her expression. It was as if she was responding to a monitor in her head. Perhaps she was, if they were all telepathic. Anyway, if this was the case, they obviously said 'go ahead, tell her' because after a moment it was clear she was going to spill the beans.

'We got here through the library,' she said. 'And it's our way back. If they close it and take out all the books it'll close our escape route and we'll be stuck here.'

'But,' I protested, remembering little paper Ryan, 'you said you were always popping in and out of other dimensions when you did your special things.'

'One or two, yes. But to get back to the one we came from we have to use the library. Do you know what wormholes are?'

This seemed an abrupt change of subject. 'What, little sort of dusty holes in the furniture?'

Archie sighed. 'Didn't you ever watch Star Trek? Wormholes in space enable you to travel enormous distances between places light years apart. You can cross lots of dimensions at the same time through similar tunnels.'

'And you're saying Oak Grove is one of them?'

'Well, the entrance to one, yes.'

'But why? How can a red brick Victorian building be a sort of departure lounge for hyperspace?' Even as I questioned it, I started to believe it, because in the back of my mind, I'd always seen the library as a gateway to other worlds. It just seemed so impossible that that's exactly what it would turn out to be.

'It's something to do with the concentration of energies,' said Archie. 'Not the sort of stuff you use and measure here, like electricity. It's hard to explain but if you can think of imagination, the kind you use to create the desert kingdom, as an energy source, then the library is a vast power station, not only supplying it but generating it and feeding off it too.'

A vague notion was stirring. 'You mean, like the way I get my ideas from books and they sort of breed new ideas, which I turn into stories ...'

'... which might one day turn into books in the library,' finished Archie.

'So when I met you in the fantasy section ...'

'I'd just arrived.'

'But, I don't understand. Where were the rest of you? And, and you talked about being in Primary school and everything.'

Archie shrugged. 'We all had to have a back story. Henrietta sorted all that out on an earlier visit, took the house, brought back some books so we could choose our names, that sort of thing. Mind you, that went a bit wrong, because Fitz decided the London A to Z was the best book to use, which is how I got lumbered with Archway. The others arrived here one by one so as not to attract suspicion. I was the last.'

'And was it a coincidence that I was there?' I asked.

'What do you think?' said Archie her expression quite grave again.

I didn't have time to think. I heard the sound of Eleanor Everett's voice outside the door and looked at Archie in horror. I'd made such progress with Mrs Everett and it would all be undone in an instant if she found me a) bunking off lessons and b) skulking in the sixth form centre, which was out of bounds to us.

Archie gave a small sigh and took hold of my hand. The next moment I was hurtling through space (and hyperspace as well). It didn't last long but it felt like nothing on earth, a whirl of light, colours, indistinct shapes and a strong desire to be sick. When I came to and opened my eyes, I was in a fact throwing up in the girls' loos. I could hear Archie talking to someone outside. I pulled the flush and staggered out of the door.

'Emily!' exclaimed Daniella, 'you look awful!'

She was standing with Archie who said naturally, as if she surfed between dimensions all the time (which, come to think of it, she did):

'Miss Lederer sent Daniella to look for us, but I told her you had been taken ill before we could get changed.' She turned to Daniella. 'I couldn't leave her like this, could I?'

I looked at myself in the mirror. I did indeed look awful. My eyes were red and I had a swollen face from the storm of tears that had burst out in the sixth form centre. Now I looked a tasteful shade of pale green after the worst bout of travel sickness I had ever experienced, even though I'd actually *travelled* only about thirty feet. My head began to throb.

'You'd better take her to the medical room,' said Daniella. 'I'll go and tell Miss Lederer what's happened.'

'Splash your face with cold water – it'll help,' said Archie as Daniella left.

'Is that right?' I said crossly. 'Is that what you do after teleporting?'

Archie laughed heartlessly. 'I'm used to it,' she said. 'Come on, you're not going to tell me a little thing like that can upset an Empress-Mage?'

I dutifully splashed my face. 'No, but it can do terrible things to an ordinary year ten student.'

'I kept telling you,' said Archie, tugging me off to see Matron. 'You're not ordinary at all.'

Ever since then I have been feeling even more sympathy with the little paper Ryan stuck to my notice-board. Now I knew what it was like to be lifted out of your proper dimension, I wasn't at all sure I liked it.

*   *   *

We had another AGOG! committee meeting that evening. I was feeling almost normal again by then. Everyone was a

81

bit excited, partly because of the success of the march and partly because we'd managed to persuade a councillor along. Not Bliss, who would make the decision, but Ms Butterfiled, who was one of our three local councillors. She was late and the committee were getting twitchy. Henrietta, who had fixed it up, was looking especially annoyed. Her grey pony-tail was bristling with pens and pencils and I was sure I could see a toothbrush in amongst them. I wondered how much eccentricity a councillor would put up with in a writer. The AGOG! supporters appeared not to mind.

'What's the matter with Henrietta?' I whispered to Archie. 'Is she going to do something?'

Archie looked worried. 'I don't know,' she whispered back. 'We don't now yet what she *can* do. It tends to manifest itself when a need arises.'

'Caroline Butterfield,' said Henrietta, 'is inexcusably late. She had better get here soon or it will be a waste of all our time.' She drummed her fingers irritably on her clipboard and I had a sudden vision of Caroline Butterfield being turned into a frog, but at that moment the doorbell rang. Henrietta relaxed. Uncle Albemarle showed in a very flustered councillor, all apologies for being late but with a wild look in her eyes that made me sure there was more to it than traffic jams.

All of a sudden I heard a voice speaking in my head. It was Archie.

'Go on. It's easy. Just open your mind and imagine you're tuning in to a radio station.'

The image of a black ridged knob came into my mind. I turned it.

'... never known anything like it. One minute sitting there finishing my coffee. The next standing in the doorstep without a hat or coat. Must ring the doctor tomorrow morning for an ...'

The knob vanished and so did the private thoughts of Councillor Butterfield. But I think telepathy must be addictive. I tuned my thoughts to Archie's and we both said simultaneously: *'Telekinesis!'*

So that was Henrietta's special skill! It was going to be very useful in the campaign. If councillors and officials refused to meet us, they were just going to be teleported wherever Henrietta wanted them to be. I watched her calmly interrogating Councillor Butterfield, who still looked thoroughly befuddled. I couldn't catch the thoughts of either of them. But I was bubbling with excitement because I had been telepathic with two different people that evening and one of them was Archie. It opened up distinct possibilities. And it was going to be a lot less risky than passing notes in chemistry.

'Of course, I fully support the library,' Ms Butterfield was saying. 'I'm a great reader myself.'

'And you have your surgeries there twice a month,' Henrietta pointed out smoothly.

'Indeed, myself and Councillors Strong and Nolan,' agreed Ms Butterfield. 'And I'm sure I speak for all of us when I say the last thing we want is for the library to close.'

'Does that mean you'll vote against the majority group's recommendation in Council?' said Lisle sharply. I had to admire her grasp of local politics in this dimension. Councillor Butterfield looked very uncomfortable.

'Let's hope it won't come to that,' she said. 'Believe me, I'm on your side.'

The rest of the meeting was more or less like the first one. Ms Butterfield didn't stay long. Portland ran her home in the van, since in spite of wittering about the traffic, she hadn't come in her car and appeared not to have a coat. The rest of us discussed tactics, which mainly consisted of stopping people in the High Street to sign our petition, recruiting more members in the library and going to lobby the councillors and their surgeries.

'I can do that,' I volunteered. 'And I can say I'm speaking for the school, if that's all right with you, Mrs Everett.'

Elegant Eleanor was wearing a new outfit, a vibrant fuchsia-pink silk blouse under a black suit. She was determined not to be overshadowed by the Powers.

'Good idea, Emily,' she said. 'Tell them how many signature you're collecting at Elm Park. I'll hand a form round the staffroom too and make all the teachers sign.'

I hadn't realised how much time all this library campaigning was going to take. What with the petition, the membership drive and the committee meetings, I had hardly enough time to keep up with my homework and violin practice, let alone have any spare in which to become the Empress-Mage. But having Archie with me most of the day and occasional glimpses of Fitzroy to sustain my fantasies (and those of just about every other female in the building from the smallest seventh year to Mrs Everett herself) somehow seemed enough, without having to slip away into the desert kingdom.

'Hey, Emma,' said Fitz, flashing his black eyes at me in the cafeteria queue one day. 'How's it going?'

'Fine,' I said. 'How are the history assignments?'

His beautiful ivory brow clouded over.

'Hard work,' he said. 'Much harder than I thought it was going to be.'

'I know,' I said. *Too bad you've had to give up time-travelling.*

Fitz jumped as if I'd said the words out loud, then gave me a most delicious smile.

'Naughty, naughty,' he said and I could just *feel* Daniella's envious expression boring into my back. I didn't need telepathy to know what *she* was thinking.

I didn't do it much, the telepathy I mean, but gradually I was beginning to stop thinking of myself as ordinary. Emily Grey was as dull as ever, but Emma Leigh was a telepath with friends from another dimension. Why, she had even flipped briefly into another one herself. Only the fifth probably, like the nursery slopes for a beginner skier, but definitely not this one. Discount the fact that the experience had been nauseatingly terrifying; Emma Leigh was clearly not a boring and predictably swotty schoolgirl.

Sixth formers kept coming up and asking me what 'we' were going to do next. They had thoroughly enjoyed the demonstration, and petition signing seemed a bit tame after waving placards and getting your picture in the papers.

'I hear there's talk of a sit-in' said Jacob Morse.

'Yes, but that's only if they actually try to shut the library,' I said. 'You know, move in with vans to take away the books.'

'Do you really think they'll do that?' asked Gabrielle, her eyes lighting up. I think she saw 'Saviour of the Library' as a role she could audition for, like Joan of Arc.

'Maybe, maybe not,' I said. 'But it wouldn't be much fun, you know. It would probably happen in January when it was very cold. They'd turn off the heaters and maybe even the water. We might not even have any loos.'

Gabrielle wrinkled her beautifully-chiselled nose.

'It's OK,' said Jacob. 'My Dad's in the building trade. He'd fix us up with portable loos.'

'And we could get our mums and dads to bring in flasks of soup and coffee,' added Daniella, who was ear-wigging as usual.

'And we would have plenty of sleeping bags and blankets,' I said. I was beginning to see how it could be a good experience, even though I was afraid of people like Dave the socialist worker taking it over and making it boring.

'My family would help too,' said Archie, 'but let's hope it doesn't come to that. The thing to do is to get Councillor Bliss to take back the proposal. If we leave it 'til they're taking the books away, it'll mean it's too late – we'll have lost.'

But I was beginning to think we might occupy the library before then. I wanted to keep the Elm Park students interested and I'd had an idea.

6

Deals within wheels

On the way back from school I called in at Oak Grove. It
was the first time I'd been in the library for pleasure, since
the campaign started. It was odd. I'd done so much
recruiting and petition-waving and planning with
committee members there that it was as if my old library
had disappeared and been replaced by a kind of war HQ.
I sneaked into the fantasy section and leaned against the
Ann McCaffreys breathing in the special smell of paper,
dust and a faint trace of spice that had always added up to
atmosphere in which anything was possible. I sank down
on to the grey carpet, clutching a Weiss and Hickman for
comfort, even though I'd read it four times.

This was it, the gateway to another dimension. In
one way it seemed totally impossible. The institutional
carpet, the metal and wood shelving system, the faint
beeping of computers as people looked things up, the
rustle of newspapers and odd hacking cough from the
quiet warm corner where the old people got together.

What was magical about that? But that was how it had always been and it had never stopped me from feeling the walls dissolve as I stepped into worlds full of dragons, armies, sorcery and chivalry.

The spicy smell grew more intense and I found myself looking at a pair of long legs in black jeans.

'Are you OK, Emily?' It was Joel, smelling delicious – he probably used Body Shop rainforest shower-gel every morning.

'Sure,' I said, standing up. 'I was just trying to remember why I wanted the library to stay open.'

He laughed sympathetically. 'I know what you mean. But you look exhausted. It's my coffee break now. Come and have some with me in the staffroom.'

I followed obediently as he led the way through a maze of musty windowless passages which led to the hidey-hole where he and Isis and the others kept their kettle and their jar of instant coffee.

'How do you like it?' he asked, spooning out the disgusting stuff.

'Oh, as it comes,' I said airily, so enchanted to be behind the scenes at Oak Grove that I didn't care if I had to drink hemlock to stay there. There was no one there but Joel and me. If only I had gone home first to change out of my school uniform!

'How's the campaigning going?' he asked as he put our mugs on the table. I took mine in both hands and nursed it, to get the benefit of the warmth. This kind didn't even *smell* nice.

'It's fine,' I said, 'but I think we need something a bit dramatic to keep people at my school interested.'

'Hmm. I see your point, but what?'

For the first time ever those gorgeous grey eyes with the extravagant lashes were trained directly at me. And he knew my name and who I was. I took a gulp of horrible coffee. After all, he *had* made it for me.

'Do you think we'd be allowed to sleep here?' I said. That certainly got Joel's attention. 'I mean sleep over on Friday nights, like a sort of sit-in,' I explained.

'But I thought that was a last resort?' said Joel. 'Something to do if they really do go through with the closure.'

'I know that's what we said we'd do,' I said, 'but I think we need practice. People at my school are dead keen on a sit-in but they don't have any idea what'll be like. If we could have some small ones before it is really necessary, then they can get a bit of experience and it'd be a way to keep them interested.

Joel looked thoughtful

'It'd bring a good deal of publicity,' he said.

'Students sleep in to save library – lots of nice-looking teenagers wrapped in blankets – but we could get into a lot of trouble. Suppose the authorities turf you out after one night? Then you might not get away with it when we really need to do it.'

'But suppose the committee agree to do it,' I said. 'Would you and Isis support us?'

'It's really Frank who you need on your side,' said Joel. Frank was the caretaker, who locked up and turned off the lights at the end of the day. He was an ex-policeman, as short as a policeman is allowed to be and he'd shrunk a bit since he retired. But in his blue shirt and navy trousers with his big jangling ring of keys, he still gave the impression of upholding the law.

'Do you think he'd be in on it?' I asked dubiously.

'Well,' said Joel. 'I don't reckon he'd be keen to start with, but he's got a soft spot for the Powers, particularly the females. Henrietta could probably get him to agree.'

He looked up at the clock (Joel never wore a watch) and said he had to get back. He took our mugs and washed them up. I was astonished to see mine was empty and I felt deeply touched at the sight of him running it under the hot tap. It was so domestic it was positively sexy.

Then he led me out through the maze again, like Theseus (though I was sure he'd never abandon me on an island if he'd promised to take me back to his kingdom). We reached the counter and Joel relieved Isis, so that she could go off for her break.

'I'd better go,' I said. 'Thanks for the coffee. Will you talk to Frank if I talk to Henrietta?'

'You bet,' said Joel. 'You're quite a firebrand when you get going, aren't you, Emily?'

I glowed all the way home, not like a firebrand, but warmed by his praise and his attention. And I was still caught up in my plan. It wasn't just that I wanted to give the Elm Park students something exciting to do. If the library really *was* a powerhouse of energy, we could start to stockpile some of it. Having a group of fifth and sixth-formers like the Elm Park lot, with all their ideas and hopes and dreams, sleeping or staying awake between the bookstacks would only build up the level of imagination-juice or whatever it was, that would help keep the Powers' gateway open.

My father thought my idea was quite mad and I thought that he was going to ban my taking part, even if the committee agreed. But Mum surprised me by saying:

'I think it's very enterprising for Emily to show such an interest in community action. It'll be good for her. She might even go on to do A-level Politics.'

And of course when I explained to Henrietta what

was behind my idea, she made sure that the committee thought it was enterprising too. So it wasn't long before Archie and I were recruiting people for the first Friday night sleep-in at Oak Grove.

'We ought to just send Fitz round with a sandwich board on him,' I said, as we saw a queue of girls, headed by Daniella, waiting to sign his list to join.

'Saying what?' said Archie.

'Come and sleep with me at Oak Grove,' I said and she grinned wickedly.

'What about recruiting the boys?' she asked.

'Fitz could probably get half of them too,' I said. 'But you could wear the sandwich board for the others.'

That first Friday was really great. I'd chosen Friday because we still have late night opening until eight o'clock, which meant all the demonstrators could have had their hot dinners at home before they came to the sleep-in. At quarter to eight everyone assembled in the foyer, with their sleeping bags, torches, flasks and carrier-bags full of breakfast. This was a kids-only protest. We carried a banner saying 'Elm Park will keep Oak Grove open' so that the last stragglers leaving the library could see what we were up to.

'Does that mean that I can change my library book in the middle of the night?' asked one wag.

At 8pm sharp, Isis left. Frank locked the doors and switched off the main lights. A constellation of torches clicked on in response. Frank wished us luck and locked up at the back. Minutes later we heard his car driving away. We were on our own. Some of the girls had brought candles and incense sticks and Archie and I patrolled to make sure they were all firmly stuck in saucers and wouldn't set fire to the books or drip wax on the carpet. Jacob Morse got out his guitar and people sang all the corny songs like 'We shall overcome' and 'Kumbaya'. Jacob and Fitz were working on a lyric for 'Where have all the bookshelves gone?'

The library must have looked very pretty from the outside with all the torches and candlelight shining through the windows. A policeman came and peered through the door, and lots of passers-by stopped and waved. At ten o'clock a reporter from the local TV news came with a camera crew and tried to interview Gabrielle through the looked door. The sound quality must have been awful but the pictures were good and we made sure the windows were full of banners and placards.

When the TV people left, the mood changed a bit. Someone had a portable radio and played music to keep our spirits up. The library was getting cold, because the heating had been turned off at half-past seven. People

94

started rolling out their sleeping bags and having hot drinks.

'Imagine what it must be like sleeping rough in the winter,' I said. Oak Grove might be chilly but it wasn't anything like sheltering from the wind and rain in a shop doorway. And it was safe. Some of the sixth-formers started telling ghost stories and those 'urban myths' like the one about the granny on the roof rack. I wondered if this would really provide the energy stocks I was hoping for.

'There's no loo paper!' whined Daniella after a quick visit to the only public cloakroom in the library, but I was ready for her and had brought a nine-pack with me.

'You're so *practical*, Emily,' said Ryan.

'All the most romantic people are,' said Fitz's sexy voice in the dark. Gradually, more and more torches were turned off and we settled down to sleep by the orange glow of the street-lights through the windows.

'No reading under the bedclothes, Emily!' said Jacob.

'Why not? She's got plenty of books to choose from,' said Gabrielle and I realised their sleeping bags were next to one another.

I rolled mine out in the fantasy section, where I felt most at home, with Archie on one side and Fitz on the other. It was ages before I could get to sleep. For a start I can't manage without a pillow and I'd forgotten to bring one. There were whispers and giggles from all the library bays. Was this going to turn into a sort of John and Yoko love-in for libraries? The publicity could backfire. Then I was terribly aware of Fitz lying a foot away from me in the dark.

I was wondering why he didn't make my heart turn over the way Joel did. He was much better looking and always flatteringly attentive to me. And K'sedra had always been secretly attracted to Prince Khalid, even though it was her throne he was after, rather than herself. Perhaps that was part of the problem; Fitz didn't seem like a real person to me. He was my own creation – too much a part of myself. It wasn't like Cathy and Heathcliff, more like Anne Rice and the Vampire Lestat. He was fascinating, my idea of the perfectly beautiful man, but that was the trouble – he *was* my idea. He couldn't surprise me. I sighed. I'd rather have horrible coffee made for me by Joel than drink champagne out of jewelled goblets with Fitz.

But I think what was actually keeping me awake was the presence of all the books. Long before I had got into fantasies, when I was small and read my way through all the Mary Poppins and Dr Dolittle books, I had felt the power of fiction, but I'd never been in the middle of it in the middle of the night before. It was as if the characters were fluttering to get out of their paper prisons. Gawain and Loki and Perseus from the myths and legends shelves, Jane Eyre, Cathy Earnshaw and Tess of the D'Urbervilles from the classic section. Heroes and heroines separated by hundreds of years, trying to close the gap.

Perhaps it was my new telepathic powers, but I spent a lot of the night feeling I was one book or another, complete with all its characters and incidents. I was sort of riding on the top of sleep all night, partly below its surface, like an unwise summer swimmer basking on a lilo. I was aware of groans and cries from other sleeping students, as if they'd all been affected by the forces of fiction that seemed to be fermenting all around us.

By seven o'clock a cold grey November light was filtering in through the big curtainless windows. Oak Grove was not a pretty sight. Grey-faced teenagers were yawning and stretching, having slept in their crumpled clothes. Everyone was complaining of weird dreams and lack of sleep and everyone was cold.

'Come on, Emma,' said Fitz. 'Time to get romantic.'

He meant 'be practical'. I moved briskly among the sleepers collecting volunteers to help make hot drinks. I led them through the maze to the secret kitchen which I'd stocked the night before with several jars of chocolate drink and a supply of Styrofoam cups. We found a tray and took steaming cups round to all the waking beauties. Everyone sat up, still in their padded sleeping bags, sipping hot chocolate and eating a variety of strange breakfasts from marmite sandwiches to apple pies. Jacob Morse was wearing a woolly hat and had grown some impressive stubble. I thought perhaps we had done Gabrielle a favour by letting her see what he looked like first thing in the morning in a 'controlled environment', as it were. But he gave her one of his crinkly grins and she rewarded him with a beautiful smile, managing somehow to look immaculately lovely.

'You're brilliant, you know, Emily,' she said to me. 'No one would have done anything about the library if you hadn't organised us all.' She stretched elegantly, like Mirza, and smiled again. 'And it's really worth it, isn't it? I couldn't bear it if they closed Oak Grove now. Not after we've slept here. It's made it sort of ours.'

This was the longest speech Gabrielle had ever addressed to me. I blushed and mumbled, but I was really pleased.

It was a real job getting everything tidied up. I'd brought bin-liners and a dustpan and brush but here were an awful lot of crumbs, candle-stubs, Styrofoam cups and paper tissues lying about the place. Smoking had been strictly banned but I still found one or two stubs. By the time we heard Frank unlocking the back door, Oak Grove had stopped looking like a doss-house and gone back to being a library. The heating came on at nine, when Isis and Joel arrived to do their Saturday shift, and by the time the doors opened to the public at half-past nine, it was warm and cosy again. The TV crew were first in, to follow up on last night's story and this time they interviewed me.

'And here is Emma Leigh Grey, the student representative on the library committee, and organiser of the protest,' said the interviewer. 'Now Emma, tell our viewers what you think you've achieved by sleeping in the library last night?'

'Well,' I swallowed. 'We were expressing student solidarity with the library staff, for a start.' I saw the camera pan over to the counter and linger on Isis in all her fresh morning gorgeousness. Then back to me. It took a real effort to remember I was Emma Leigh, the dashing campaigner. I wished I'd brought my toothbrush. 'And we wanted everyone to know how much we care,' I plunged on. 'We're all doing our exams and we couldn't manage without the library.'

A chorus of cheers broke out behind me and the students raised our banner. It gave me courage.

'And it's not just school students who need it,' I continued. 'It's important for the elderly and for small children.'

Several pensioners were obligingly homing in on the newspapers and a stream of littlies was going into the children's library. They had been carefully orchestrated by Henrietta and Lisle but it still made excellent TV pictures.

I watched the coverage at the Powerhouse that lunchtime.

'Excellent, Emma Leigh,' said Henrietta.

'Yes, well done,' said Lisle.

'I think we're going to win,' said Portland.

'I've been wondering,' I said cautiously, not knowing quite how far to go with a whole roomful of Powers. 'If you're so worried, you know, about not getting back if the library closes, why don't you go before the decision is made?' My fingers were tightly crossed, because I lived in dread of their sudden disappearance. But I had to know.

'I don't know how much Archway has told you about our reasons for coming here,' said Portland, equally carefully. It was as if we were both picking our way across broken glass.

'She said you were being persecuted,' I said, looking at huge Portland and the muscular uncles. They didn't look like victims.

'Not a bad word for it,' said Portland. 'If we continue to use terms from this dimension, you might say we're dissidents.'

'You mean you disagree with your government?' I asked. I couldn't imagine what kind of governments other dimensions might have.

'Yes, as long as you realise that "government" is a metaphor,' said Portland. 'You know that there are a lot of beings with great powers in our universe. Wherever there is power, there is also abuse of power. We tried to stop some of our number from abusing their powers and we were hounded for it.'

I was relieved. I hadn't believed that they could have committed a crime but I had been worrying about why they'd left their dimension. 'Dissidents' seemed all right, almost respectable.

'How can you ever go back then?' I asked.

'We have to wait for ... let's call it a change of government,' said Portland. 'In those terms, it is not yet safe for us to return. But we still hope that day will come. And when it does, we'll need the library to be there.'

I gave up. I could only take a certain amount of weirdness, even if my threshold was higher than most people's. After thinking about the Powers as extra-terrestrials for any length of time, my mind just clicked back to seeing them as a family; it was kind of matter over mind thing. They just *looked* so human.

My next job on the campaign front was to go to the councillors' surgery at the library on Monday evening. All day at school people kept coming up to me and asking if we were going to have another sleep-in that Friday. Word had got around that it was the cool thing to do: Jacob and Gabrielle now walked openly round the school hand in hand and I think a lot of sixth formers were beginning to see the library as an offbeat pick-up joint. A lot of people stopped to say they had seen me on TV. Even Mrs Everett referred to me in English as 'our media celebrity' but you could tell she wasn't being catty.

Mum grumbled a bit about my going to the surgery, even though she was off to evening class herself.

'You're spending more time at the library than you are home these days,' she complained. It was on the tip of my tongue to say the same her about the Education Centre, but Dad gave me a warning look.

I had to wait ages to see the councillors. There was a long queue of old ladies in woolly hats (I swear they clone them in Oak Grove) and one or two unemployeds not much older than me. I stood there shifting from one foot to another listening to the querulous tones of people wanting their rents frozen or their pipes thawed and drifted off into the desert kingdom.

> I was listening to the petitions of my subjects in the marble stateroom of the sapphire palace.
> 'Give justice, Your Resplendence, to your humble servant, I pray you. For that my neighbour has unlawfully and with malice taken my best camel from me.'
> I looked up towards my vizier ...

To my amazement I saw that he was one of the uncles, the red curls were unmistakable. I was quite sure that he hadn't looked like that the last time I was in the palace and, as if to confirm, this was an invasion, the *vizier* winked. Anyone who knows anything about this kind of story knows that viziers never wink. Sneer maybe, even grimace, but not wink.

I opened my eyes and found myself at the head of the queue. The three councillors, Butterfield, Nolan and Strong were sitting at separate tables in the meetings room. They had been dealing with people three at a time, but I was the last, so they sort of pushed their tables together and faced me like a bench of magistrates. It may have been intended to unnerve me; that was certainly the effect. I think Councillor Butterfield remembered me but I'd never seen the other two before. Nolan looked quite friendly but Strong had a cold and steely look about him that I associated with desert spies.

'I've come about the library,' I plunged in.

'An, yes,' said Strong with a vizier-like sneer. 'I saw you on television. And I must say I think occupying the library was a highly irrational and unnecessary act. We deplore such scaremongering tactics.'

'Hang on, Ken,' said Councillor Nolan. 'Let the lass have her say and don't talk as if we all thought the same. It looked like good fun to me – like one of those sixties love-ins.'

Councillor Strong wrinkled his long nose in distaste but kept quiet. I told them that I was representing the whole school and that people felt very strongly about the library. We had petition signatures from all the staff and about two thirds of the students so far. We weren't going to let the matter drop; the library was now a high profile issue. Nolan leaned forward, really interested, and kept asking questions. But more than once I saw Caroline Butterfield and Ken Strong exchanging glances above his head. I didn't know if my new skills would work when there was no Power beside me, but I gradually tuned out what Councillor Nolan was saying and focused on what

Councillor Butterfield was thinking. I'd invaded her mind before so I thought it might be easier than Strong's.

At first I thought it wasn't working; it wasn't like before when I tuned a knob and got her thoughts like a radio station. This was more like TV; I got a picture of a letter on council note paper. It was addressed to Councillor Strong and signed by Alan Bliss. I pressed silently, trying to discover where the letter was. Caroline shifted uncomfortably, but I got my answer. A mental picture of Strong's briefcase.

'… don't you see?' Councillor Nolan was asking.

I had no idea what he had been saying but was saved from admitting it by a voice behind me.

'Good evening, Councillors, I've come to walk Emma Leigh home. I think she's taken up enough of your time.'

I looked round and saw Albemarle Power, the flute player. His left eye dropped for a micro-second and I knew he'd been sent to help me. Whatever it was he could do, his skills were needed now.

'There's a letter from Bliss in Strong's briefcase,' I said to him silently. 'Is there anything you can do about it?'

Albemarle let his gaze dwell for a moment on Strong's black attaché-case, while exchanging pleasantries with the councillors.

'Got it,' came into my mind. 'Let's get out of here quickly.'

And we clattered off down the stairs past Frank jangling his keys.

'What was it?' I asked out loud. 'And what did you do?'

Albemarle looked up and down the stairs, then whispered, 'X-Ray vision. It could come in quite handy, couldn't it?'

'How did you find out?' I asked.

'Some labels came off cans in the larder,' he said sheepishly. 'I just looked at them and *saw* what was inside. Then Lisle said you needed me, so I came.'

'What was in the letter?'

'A deal,' said Albemarle grimly. 'Bliss has agreed to cut the library so Strong can have funds for a project of his, some leisure centre or something. It appears Strong has some kind of hold over him.'

'What does it mean?' I said, alarmed.

'It means,' said Albemarle, 'that Bliss has already decided to close the library. And if that happens, we'll be stranded here forever.'

7

Unfair advantages

'Will you please stop going on about the way things are done at the Powers'?'

My mother had reached the end of her tether. I knew I'd been a bit of a Power bore for the last few weeks, but I hadn't realised how far it had gone. The last straw was when I criticised her casserole.

'If you want to become a vegetarian, fine,' she continued. 'Lots of teenagers do. But I haven't got time to make you separate meals. I'll buy you a cook book and you can make your own.' With that parting shot, she gathered up her books and files and flounced off to another evening class. Dad I washed up in silence. I had a lot more on my mind than diet.

If Albemarle was right, and the library was doomed, I couldn't see anything for it but for the Powers to leave now. Whatever awaited them in their dimension couldn't be worth the risk of getting trapped here. So they'd go and my life would revert to its world of greys and sludges, made a hundred times duller because of the burst of colour and excitement that had briefly invaded it. And if that wasn't enough, there'd no longer be my fastness with Joel and Isis to retreat into. I was heading for a very bleak midwinter indeed.

Next morning, Mrs Everett collared me as soon as I got into school, but even being sought out by the school's most charismatic teacher didn't raise my spirits.

'Are you having another sleep-in at Oak Grove this Friday?' she asked immediately. 'Because remember we've got the Majority group meeting on Monday and it would keep the PR profile up.'

'I'm not sure there's any point,' I said. 'The Powers have found something out.' I had to be careful here. 'It seems that Councillor Bliss has already made the decision to close the library. They think he may have been blackmailed into it.'

Mrs Everett gave me an icy stare. 'So that's it, is it? Roll over and waggle our legs in the air? Do the words "civil rights" mean nothing to you? Freedom of information? Democracy? Really, Emily, I thought better of you. But if you're wimping out on me, I'd better find Gabrielle.' She turned on her high heels and rode off on her high horse.

'*Oh bum!*' I thought. '*I can't lose Mrs Everett along with everything else.*' I pelted after her.

'Mrs Everett! I'm sorry. I was just feeling a bit disheartened. You know, all the important decisions being made in smoke-filled rooms by the big guys?'

She had stopped and was tapping her plum-coloured fingernails against a black folder.

'Do you know your bible, Emily?' she asked.

'You mean David and Goliath?'

'I was thinking more of Samson and Delilah,' she said. 'Get them where they're vulnerable. If Councillor Bliss is being blackmailed he must have done something dodgy. We need to find out what. I'll give Lisle a ring. Meanwhile, the fight must go on.'

'Yes,' I said, brightening. 'If we keep on doing the same thing it might even make Bliss think we don't know anything new.'

'Very perceptive,' nodded Mrs Everett. 'I knew I could count on you.' She gave me one of her special conspiratorial smiles and swept off, trailing clouds of Armani behind her.

Nearly everyone was game for another sleep-in. It was now definitely cool to support the library. A few wimps who had complained about being cold and uncomfortable said they wouldn't do it again but they were more than made up for by the number of newcomers who'd thought it would compromise their image last time. I was getting better at thinking ahead and deciding what we'd need. Everyone was given a list of things to bring, including hot-water bottles. The new recruits thought that was very uncool and made silly remarks about other ways to keep warm, so I blessed Gabrielle and Jacob for slapping them down.

'If you'd spent one night in that morgue, you'd know why she says bring hot-water bottles,' said Jacob. 'And I'm as hot-blooded as the next man.' He gave Gabrielle a big bear-hug.

Archie was worried. Obviously Albemarle had told her about the letter but, strangely enough, that didn't seem to bother her as much as I thought it would.

'What's up?' I asked, during lunch. Archie looked round as if she expected invaders from another dimension to materialise in the canteen.

'I don't think we're going to get anywhere just by sleeping in the library and waving banners outside the Town Hall,' she said.

'That's what I told Eleanor,' I said, 'and she told me off for being defeatist, said we should find a way of cutting

Councillor Bliss's hair.'

'But he's bald,' objected Archie.

'It's a metaphor,' I sighed. 'You ought to know all about that. You're practically one yourself.'

'Thanks,' said Archie, sarcastically. (*I'd* have been genuinely grateful if anyone ever said anything like that to me. Only they wouldn't of course). 'What I mean is, I think we're going to have to find out more about this behind-the-scenes deal. And I don't see how we can do it without using our – you know – unfair advantages.'

'So what?' I said. 'Who cares about being unfair to them? Bliss is going to take away our library, just to keep his name out of the papers.'

'Oh, I don't care about being unfair,' said Archie. 'It's just that I'm worried about giving ourselves away. We seem to have got away with it so far, but every time one of us does something that isn't strictly possible in this world it's like sending out a flare saying "Yoohoo! Over here!"'

'You're definitely not thinking about going back there?' I asked.

'Definitely,' said Archie. 'It's too dangerous.'

I sighed. My brain, although adept at entering and creating new worlds, couldn't encompass what kind of creature could threaten beings as strong and gifted as the Powers.

'You surely don't want us to go?' asked Archie. 'Look, you know that asylum case that's been in all the papers?'

'You mean the man who says he'll be killed if he goes back, so he's hiding in a church in Bolton?'

'Yes, the one we heard about at the last Amnesty meeting. The dissident who's already had six members of his family eliminated by his government. Well, it's like that. We'd be mad to go back there until we'd heard it was safe.'

'So you're asylum seekers, are you?' Portland hadn't put it like that.

'Not exactly,' admitted Archie. 'We didn't ask anyone's permission, except perhaps yours.'

I snorted. 'You call invading my brain and inhabiting my fantasies asking permission?'

Archie grinned her wicked grin. 'It was better than trying to get inside the Home Secretary's head.'

We shuddered dramatically.

'OK, what's the plan then?' I asked. 'I mean, I assume you're worrying about this because you're planning to do something noticeable?'

She told me.

'All right,' I said slowly. 'It could work. But only if you take me with you.'

To say our next sleep-in went like clockwork is putting it mildly; it went like liquid crystal. You know how the second time you do something it can feel as if you've been doing the same thing at regular intervals all your life? We had already developed little rituals and traditions. The number of boys in woolly hats and fingerless gloves was a tribute to Jacob's power as a role model. And more than one of them had a guitar this time, too. The camaraderie was really good and made up for the lack of heating. We all settled down to sleep much later than before.

Another tradition quickly established was that Fitz and Archie and I would all sleep in the same place. This was actually vital to our plan, as well as being prestigious for me, but it was very nearly blighted by Daniella. She and quite a few other girls would have liked unrolling their sleeping bags alongside the adorably Byronic Fitzroy. If Grove sleep-ins were to be about people getting together, Fitz was certainly the male most Elm Park girls wanted to get together with.

'Can I sleep here with you, Emily?' Daniella said, dragging her sleeping bag behind her like an insomniac Christopher Robin. I noticed incredulously that she had changed into a satin-look nightshirt. She looked like Victoria Beckham with goose pimples.

'Daniella, you'll freeze like that,' I said sharply. 'Put

something else on immediately.'

Daniella pouted. 'You sound like my mother. But can I sleep here? It's much cosier in this bay than out in the main library.'

'There's no room,' said Archie unkindly.

'Yes there is, there's plenty of room,' argued Daniella, trying to squeeze in between me and Fitz. This was disastrous.

'Do something,' I mindspoke to both Powers. Fitz leapt to his feet.

'I can't sleep so close to you, Daniella,' he said gallantly, 'not dressed like that. I'll just go and lie down somewhere out there.' He gave her a wonderful mixture of rueful smile and smouldering look, which by torchlight was quite something. Frankly I didn't think this was going to work.

'But you sleep next to Emily,' Daniella objected uncertainly.

'Emma Leigh is like a sister to me,' said Fitz. Daniella trailed off, believing herself irresistible to Fitz's hormones. I managed to give him a satisfying kick in the dark.

'Ryan!' we heard her whispering. 'Where are you?'

'That was close,' said Archie. 'Do you think any more of your groupies will notice your absence, Fitz?'

'Not unless they come looking for him in the middle of the night,' I said.

Fitz gave me a wolfish grin. 'Daniella will probably tell them you're my bodyguard.'

Gradually the whispers and giggles subsided out in the main library, the torches were extinguished and the candles guttered. We didn't need light for what we were going to do. Archie moved stealthily between me and Fitz and took our hands.

I was prepared this time. I had been taking Kwells every two hours all afternoon. Perhaps it was the pills or perhaps I was just getting better at teleporting, but at least I wasn't sick when we arrived, although I did feel that all my molecules had been taken apart and reassembled by someone who'd lost the instruction manual.

We were in the garden of a house I'd never seen. I clung weakly on to Archie while Fitz peered through the front window.

'What can you see?' asked Archie.

'Nothing,' Fitz replied silently. *'It's too dark. But it is number 63.'*

He manoeuvred himself into the middle position between Archie and me.

'Are you ready for phase two?' he asked me. I nodded. The leaves on the grass stirred as if a wind were blowing

and I felt suddenly tugged backwards. I closed my eyes and held on to Fitz's hand as hard as if I'd been Daniella. Was this how women in the romances she reads felt, shortly before murmuring 'my hero' and passing out?

When the turbulence stopped, and I thought it was safe to open my eyes, I found it was broad daylight. A large tree stood in the front garden about an inch from where we were; we were very lucky not to have time-travelled our way straight into it. Apart from that, the house didn't look very different.

'What do we do now?' I asked, proud of my ability to stand upright.

'We break in,' said Fitz quietly, pointing at where the burglar alarm had been in the present. In this past there was nothing but brickwork. The tree – which was full of leaves, so it wasn't winter in this time - provided excellent cover for Fitz, as he fiddled with the window.

'Damn!' he exclaimed. 'It's locked. Archie, let's not waste time. Take us in.'

I was a bit disappointed to break and enter by supernatural means – which will tell you how blasé I'd become recently – because I remembered what an expert thief Prince Khalid had always been. Still, I was glad to be out of view of the street and safely hidden in the hall. A brief reconnoitre located a room that could only be the study. On the bureau stood a photograph of a very much younger councillor Bliss and what must have been his wife, unless he made a habit of going round with women in white dresses and veils clutching huge bouquets. It made me feel a bit sorry for him; after all, he was an ordinary human being like the rest of us. Well, like me anyway. I suddenly began to fee a bit sick after all.

'Think of the library,' said Archie, but I don't think she was being any more telepathic than an ordinary friend would be.

We searched systematically through all Bliss's papers. I don't know how the Powers had decided what month and year to go back to, or even how they knew Alan Bliss had lived in the same house then as he did now. But I had enough to worry about – how would we know when we'd found anything? Would our absence be discovered by prowling females in the library? I just had to trust that Archie and Fitz had got that bit right.

'Nothing here,' said Fitz, at the filing cabinet. 'It's all deadly boring committee minutes and so forth. I don't know how anyone can stand being a politician. It's so *dull*.'

'They like the power,' said Archie, who was doing the desk. 'You should understand that.'

'Hang on a minute,' I said. 'I think we're doing this

the wrong way. If there was something incriminating, he wouldn't just keep it in a file marked "Evidence", would he? Wouldn't he have hidden it somewhere secret?'

We looked for secret drawers, a safe behind a picture, that sort of thing. Fitz was getting worried.

'We've been here nearly two hours. Suppose someone comes back?'

I was going systematically through the bookcase. It was made of cheap laminated composition board and kept upright only by the weight of the books. They were deadly dull, all about local government, not a single fantasy among them. I took each one out, shook it and put it back. I was on the bottom shelf fluttering the pages of Bentwell's *Housing Policy and Building Regulations*, when a piece of paper fell to the floor. I thought it was probably only a newspaper cutting or something being used as a bookmark. But as soon as I picked it up, I knew we'd hit the jackpot. It was a memorandum from Councillor Bliss authorising the sale of a council-owned building. Stapled to it was a letter dated 17th June 1983 from a property developer. It just said 'Thank you for the information received. Our cheque is in the post.'

'What an idiot!' said Fitz. 'Why would he keep something like this?'

'Maybe he was just keeping it till the cheque arrived

and forgot to throw it away?' suggested Archie.

'We can check if it did arrive,' I said. 'He keeps his bank statements in this drawer in the bureau.' I riffled through until I found the one for June. 'Look! There's a huge payment in on the twenty-fifth. Five thousand pounds!'

Fitzroy frowned. 'Is it enough?'

'Sounds enough to me,' I said. 'Five grand in the early eighties wasn't anything to sneeze at.'

'NO, I mean enough to blackmail him with,' said Fitz.

'He could always say it was a present from his granny or something.'

'I think it's what we're looking for,' said Archie. 'We've got the letter and the memo. And Strong might have something more.'

'What did he do exactly?' asked Fitz.

'He was Chair of the Housing Committee then,' I said, looking at the memo. 'He must have let this property developer know that he was going to advise the Council to sell the building and the property developer must have got in early with a low bid. Maybe he got such a good deal, it was worth slipping Bliss a five grand back-hander.'

'OK,' said Archie, 'we'd better hurry. Is that thing a photocopier?'

'Why?' I asked. 'Can't we just take the originals?'

Fitz gave me a mock-horrified look. 'Don't you know about tampering with the fabric of the space-time continuum, Emma Leigh?'

'No, I don't,' I said crossly.

'There isn't time to explain now,' said Archie. 'Just take our word for it that unpredictable things can happen if you move objects from one time and place to another. It's safer to take copies.'

The 'thing' she had referred to didn't look like the photocopier in the library and the paper felt funny but it did make copies of the memo, the letter and the bank statement. We had just finished putting everything back when we heard the front door opening. Fitz grabbed me by one arm and Archie grabbed me by the other. Before I had time to protest the world started spinning and I felt myself being sucked into a kind of tunnel with muscles. It was like being swallowed.

I came to in the dark with a terrible headache. Both my arms were still being held, I breathed out as slowly as I could and asked: 'Was that teleporting or time-travel?'

'Both,' said Fitzroy.

'Sorry,' said Archie. 'No time to consult. Are you all right?'

'I will be if I can get some sleep,' I said. 'I take it we're back in the library?'

'Yes,' said Fitz and gingerly turned his torch on, away from the main party of sleepers, and shone it on the books.

I yawned. 'Tell me that no time passed at all while we were away,' I begged. Fitz shone the torch on his watch.

'Only about thirty seconds,' he said. 'We'd have only been rumbled if someone had looked at that instant.'

I crawled into my sleeping bag, snuggled up to my lukewarm hot-water bottle and was asleep as soon as my head crashed on to the pillow (I had remembered one this time).

*   *   *

I was woken by a loud thumping on the front door. So was everyone else. The heating had come on so we must have slept late. I, and several other students, waddled to the door in our sleeping bags. We looked as if we were taking part in a sack race. A strange man was calling through the letter-box.

'Is there a Miss E. Grey here?' he asked when I hove into his line of vision. I obviously still had the bonnet-image, even when wearing a sleeping-bag.

'That's me,' I said.

'I need to serve you with this injunction personally,' said the man, poking a brown envelope tantalisingly through the letter-box, like a burglar using a piece of steak to sweet-talk his way round an Alsatian.

'Um, no thank you,' I said, realising I didn't have to accept it.

'Just a minute,' said Jacob, struggling out of his sleeping bag. 'You can't serve an injunction on Emily at all. She's under-age.' Jacob was going to read law at university. 'You have to be eighteen, don't you?' he said to the letter-box. 'Emily's not yet fifteen.'

The brown envelope was abruptly withdrawn. After a few moments the man's voice said, 'Don't go away. I'll be back.'

'What's the injunction for?' asked Jacob.

'To get you to go away,' the voice trailed off in the distance.

Jacob and I looked at one another and everyone burst out laughing. There was around of applause.

Jacob, grinning, said, 'Council nil, Elm Park students one.'

I went off to make the hot chocolate, feeling the campaign was turning in our favour at last.

8

Ugly

We didn't hear any more from the injunction man. Jacob was a bit worried because he and some of the others would turn eighteen before Christmas. There were one or two sleepers-over who were that age already, but they had nothing to do with the organising and it would have been difficult for the Council to find out their names. My father still wasn't happy about my spending Friday nights at the library. He thought it was probably breaking the law.

'But we're not entering the building illegally,' I protested. 'We're just not leaving it at eight o'clock.'

'Then it's probably the librarians who are breaking the law,' he went on, unperturbed, 'or the caretakers for not insisting that you leave.'

I thought of ex-policeman Frank and wondered if he'd be prepared to get arrested for us. The next Friday was going to be hard.

* * *

But before then, there was the Majority Group meeting. I don't know much about local government and what I do know bores me rigid, but I did understand that this meeting was even more important than the first one. The leader of the Council and the other councillors in his party were going to discuss the budget, what was to be cut and what was to be saved, and the cuts would be agreed on. Then the proposal would go forward to the whole Council for a final vote. Since the Majority Group *were* the majority, anything they voted for would actually happen. But the meeting wasn't open to the public, and wasn't even officially happening at all.

All the petition-signing, lobbying, letter-writing and sleeping-in had been geared towards swinging the views of the Majority Group councillors before the Monday meeting. Henrietta had written to every single one of them, trying to get them to see that they would be penalising the very people they had been elected to protect: the children whose families couldn't afford to buy books, the young students who had no space or peace at home to work in, the old people and the unemployed who came to the library for warmth and someone to talk to and the people who needed help and information about their rights. It was a brilliant, passionate letter and I wondered what they'd all think if they knew the writer could have just removed them from their homes and offices without their permission and whirled them through hyperspace to her own living-room for a jolly good talking to.

The local paper and TV coverage had been full of the library campaign for weeks and, with the last sleep-in, AGOG! had hit the national news too. A *Guardian* reporter had interviewed Henrietta, Eleanor, Gabrielle and Isis. She hadn't talked to me and my name didn't appear in her article but there were photographs and quotations from all four of those beautiful women in Monday's *Guardian*. The World at One radio programme had done a telephone interview with Henrietta too and it seemed definite that the national TV news channels would turn out to cover the evening's demonstration.

Although the Majority Group meeting was unofficial, all the protest groups knew about it and it looked as if it was going to be much bigger demo than the first one. To be honest, I was a bit worried about it. There was a bit of bad feeling between some of the other interest groups and AGOG!. I think they thought we were a bit too good at generating publicity and they were jealous of all the column inches we were getting. I was worried that if they started arguing with our lot, Dave and his mates in the SWP, who had been lying low recently, would see it as a perfect excuse for a fight. We were going to have all kinds of vulnerable people from babies to old ladies in our group and I could see all sorts of problems looming.

There was no march this time. We were going to get straight down to the serious business of yelling outside the Town Hall. The Powers had made some special placards that were going to show Councillor Bliss we meant business. The weather had turned freezing cold. I tugged thick socks on over my jeans and pushed them into my boots. I pulled two pairs of gloves on and woolly hat of my own. Glancing in the mirror in the hall on the way out, I wondered if it was clear that I was wearing it like Jacob and not like a premature Emily Grey version of the little old lady squad.

As soon as I put my nose outside the door, I saw we had another problem. It had already been dark for a couple of hours and now there was a freezing fog as well. It seeped into my bones, through all my layers of clothing, and by the time I reached the Town Hall I couldn't feel my fingers, toes or nose. The fog had brought the numbers down and the dangers up. Far fewer very young or very old library supporters than usual had turned out on this filthy night. There were plenty of demonstrators, but they were all teenagers and young grown-ups and they all looked fighting fit. Some miserable-looking sound and cameramen were huddled in the back of their van. The cold was putting everyone in a foul mood.

I joined the Powers, who were all clustered together. They let me into their group and I found they were discussing the weather.

'It's not natural,' Lisle was saying.

'Yes it is,' I said. 'You may not have experienced late November in Britain before, but I have. I can assure you it's always like this.'

'What a country!' said Henrietta.

'What a dimension,' whispered Fitz in my ear.

'Can any of you do anything about it?' I whispered. It was amazing how Fitz could look like a model in a jeans ad, even when wearing a woolly hat – no danger of his being mistaken for a little old lady.

'We've been trying,' said Portland. 'That's what's worrying. With our combined capabilities, we ought to be making some impression on the visibility or the temperature – but see for yourself.'

Fog was rolling round the Town Hall steps, like dry ice filling a pantomime stage. The yellow street-lights and the illumination from the Town Hall windows reflected back off the mist, turning a ghostly glare on to the faces of the protestors. It made me more uneasy than ever, knowing there was something the Powers *couldn't* do. It was almost as unsettling as thinking about all the things they could.

'Here comes Bliss!' shouted a sharp-eyed protestor. There was a surge forwards, like the one you get at a gig when the main act comes on. I felt myself carried with the crowd, people packed around me, moving me whether I wanted to go or not. I got separated from the Powers, but I saw what happened. They had to get really close to Bliss or he wouldn't have seen them in the fog. They whipped out their placards. I saw ones saying BLISS HAS SOLD OAK GROVE! and SAVE THE LIBRARY – NOT YOUR SKIN!

Bliss went mad. Portland and the uncles towered over him but the bald little man went right up to them and hissed in their faces. I couldn't hear what he said, though I'm sure I caught the word 'libel'. I couldn't quite see the Powers' faces either. The fog swirled round Bliss's shoulders like a magician's cape. Something about him had changed. He was still a small, bald-headed, insignificant-looking man, but now he seemed charged with emotion and quite frightening.

The TV men were frantic, trying to get a camera and a sound boom and mike near enough to get footage of the confrontation. One of them must have trodden on a swimming-pool demonstrator's foot, because he tried to deck the cameraman with his placard (HOW LOW CAN YOU SINK?). Unfortunately, he missed and clocked one of

Dave's cronies, who immediately retaliated with a swift kick from his tartan DM.

All of a sudden punches were being thrown and the demo had deteriorated into an all-out brawl. The TV people got very excited, filming everything. Their reporter, a young woman with shoulder-length marmalade-coloured hair and a sheepskin jacket, was desperately trying to talk into her mike. The uncles were each holding a flailing demonstrator by the collar. Then I caught sight of Mrs Everett. Her face was deathly pale and streaked with bright red blood. I guessed it was her own, because her eyes rolled up into her head and I saw her sink into the crush.

'Portland!' I screamed. 'Mrs Everett's hurt!'

A presence like a bear forced its way through the mess of bodies and lifted a limp Eleanor above the heads of the crowd.

'Ambulance!' roared Portland. The TV reporter dropped her mike and reached for her mobile phone. I loved her for that. I saw Eleanor open her eyes, find them level with Portland's red beard and close them with a shudder.

Soon the Town Hall steps were swarming with policemen; cars were arriving with blue lights flashing and sirens screaming. This was more excitement than Lark Hill

Forest had known for generations. Dave and several of his friends were arrested but seemed quite cheerful about it. I saw them giving a variety of military salutes as they were shoved into a police van. The van sped away, followed by the ambulance with Eleanor Everett in it, its flashes and wails adding to the general *son et lumière* effect. I was pretty sure she had nothing worse than a scalp wound.

I was feeling rather bashed about myself by then. No one had attacked me but I had been squeezed, trodden on and elbowed. I'd lost my placard and my hat. I couldn't see any of the Powers and all of a sudden I felt like crying. Everything had turned ugly.

'Emily!' said a familiar voice and Joel appeared through the fog. I flung myself into his arms and sobbed. 'There, there,' he said awkwardly, patting my shoulders. 'Are you all right? Has anyone hurt you?'

'No,' I snuffled pathetically. 'I was just frightened. But it's OK now you're here.' Oh K'sedra, how you have fallen!

'Let's get you out of here,' said Joel, taking the situation in hand and glancing over his shoulder. It was then that I saw he had someone with him, a small woman with gleaming honey-coloured hair. (Why do all these good-looking woman have hair the colour of things you can spread on toast? The closest mine gets is peanut butter.) I burned with embarrassment. My ears heard Joel say, 'Emily, this is Catherine.' My brain translated: 'Emily, you have made an idiot of yourself in front of my girlfriend.'

Catherine was lovely. Not stunningly pretty (apart from her hair) but warm and friendly and very concerned. Together they took me to the Coffee Bean and fed me sweet hot chocolate. I think I must have been in shock, but I can't say whether it was because of the violence or the realisation that Joel wasn't unattached after all. Naturally I let Catherine believe the first.

'Sorry,' I kept saying. 'I'm not usually such a wimp, am I, Joel?'

'Emily is brave as a lion, as clever as a fox and as efficient as a beaver,' he said, smiling his gorgeous lopsided smile. My heart turned over. Such a menagerie of compliments, all useless now. I could feel my extremities again but my heart was completely numb: the bit of me that had feelings – of jealousy, of longing, of huge sadness – was frozen. I knew it was going to thaw out as soon as I was alone and that I would cry myself to sleep but for now all my energies were concentrated on convincing Joel and, even more, Catherine, that I was perfectly fine, never better.

By the time we left the café, my smile felt stitched on to my face. They insisted on giving me a lift home in

Joel's red Beetle – the times I had imagined being run home in that chariot of desire! The door was opened by a very worried Dad. I waved goodbye to my rescuers, then my mouth sagged and I felt a huge lump rising under my polo neck.

'Emily!' said Dad in that cross voice parents use when they're really relieved. 'Are you all right? We saw the demonstration on television. It was terrifying. I rang the police.'

'I'm fine, Dad,' I said in a treacherously wobbly voice. 'You'd better ring them again. It was scary but nothing happened to me. I'm just cold and tired.'

'Was that young man who brought you home the librarian? The one with the long hair?'

'Yes,' I said. 'That was Joel. He and his girlfriend took me for a hot drink. They were very nice.'

Dad gave me a sympathetic look. 'If I were you, 'I'd have a hot bath and get to bed. You look all in.'

I didn't need telling twice. As I sank into the bubbles, the hot water found new bruises and scratches I didn't know I had. My brain played its own newsreel of the demo. The campaign had gone several steps backwards this evening. Everything had started to go wrong from the moment Bliss had turned up. I couldn't understand his reaction; he hadn't seemed at all afraid of the Powers' accusations. Surely we hadn't been wrong about his shady dealings at Housing or his deal with Councillor Strong?

Carefully, I dried myself and, swaddled in my warm purple pyjamas and woolly dressing-grown, sat on the edge of my bed, taking deep breaths and brushing my hair. The Empress-Mage had two slaves to brush her hair, but then it was waist-length with the texture of silk and the colour of midnight ...

K'sedra woke at dawn the morning after her confrontation with the armies over the mountains. Her bodyguard roused her slaves, who made as if to brush her hair, but she dismissed them and, tying her sable tresses back in a simple knot, stepped out into the warm scented air of the palace gardens. The atmosphere was washed clean by the heavy spring rains and there was a feeling of renewal.

K'sedra was restless in spite of sleeping well. The bodyguard followed at a discreet distance while she made her way to the outer wall and climbed the battlements. Dawn broke as she reached the top and the red sun of Krin rose balefully into the sky. K'sedra caught her breath.

In the night, the desert had bloomed. While K'sedra had slept on in her royal bed, as soundly as a peasant-girl, the annual miracle of her arid kingdom had happened without her knowledge. In the palace gardens, there were flowers all the year round, but in the kingdom at large, outside the palace walls, it was only after the miserable downpour of the spring rains that the scrubland suddenly blossomed with vivid-coloured flowers.

'At last,' murmured K'sedra and sent a watchman to bring her the brightest bloom ...

With a jerk, I came to and found myself not in Krin, nor even in my bedroom. I was in the Powers' living-room, still holding my hairbrush. Now I knew exactly how Councillor Butterfield must have felt, but for me outrage outweighed bewilderment. I knew exactly how I had got there.

I glared at Henrietta icily. 'You do realise I was in the bath a few minutes ago, don't you?'

They were all there, watchful and guarded. At least Henrietta had transported me to the rug in front of the fireplace. Lisle's dried sunflowers had been replaced by a blazing log-fire. Fitz had his long legs stretched out in front of it. He now had a black eye to match his piratical curls.

'You look much sexier in your night things than Daniella does,' he said.

'Shut up, Fitz,' I said crossly. I was in no mood to be flattered or flirted with. In fact I had been wondering whether to make K'sedra a celibate Empress-Mage, like the Virgin Queen.

'I'm sorry to bring you here so unceremoniously,' said Henrietta. 'But we have a serious problem.'

'Yeah,' I said. 'Fitz's beauty isn't what it was. Why doesn't one of you fix it?'

'What's the matter, Emma Leigh?' They all mindspoke at the same time, their voices overlapping in my brain like rustling leaves. My crossness evaporated. Whether they were people, superhumans or coloured blobs, the Powers were on my side. I carefully made a little box in my mind and put all my feelings for Joel in it and stuck a big label on it saying PRIVATE, KEEP OUT! The Powers' minds edged away from it and they sent me a strong surge of sympathy.

'OK, OK,' I said briskly out loud. 'I'm all right now. I was very tired and was just going to bed when you whisked me here. So can you just tell me what this is about and whisk me back? I need my beauty sleep.'

'It's Councillor Bliss,' said Grosvenor.

'Yeah. What did he say?' I asked.

'It wasn't exactly what he *said*,' said Albemarle uneasily. 'It's more a question of what he *is*.'

'Bald? Middle-aged? A councillor?' I hazarded. These didn't really seem dangerous characteristics to me, but at the same time I remembered that there *had* been something different about Bliss.

'You remember the fog?' asked Portland, as if it had happened ten years ago.

'I told you,' I said. 'We always get fog in November. We're famous for it – Sherlock Holmes, Charles Dickens, *An American Werewolf in London*.'

'OK,' said Archie. 'Where is it now?'

'What do you mean?' I said stupidly. 'Outside, of course.'

Lisle turned off the single standard lamp and went over to the long windows and pulled back the shutters. Moonlight flooded the room. It was a cold crisp night with lots of stars. A single street-light shone clear across the street. I shrugged. 'British weather is notoriously changeable.'

'Emma Leigh,' said Henrietta firmly. 'This was no ordinary change in the weather. Bliss brought the fog with him.'

'And he brought the bad feelings that broke up the demonstration,' added Lisle.

'What are you saying?' I asked. 'That Bliss is some kind of weather-mage?'

'Very possible,' said Portland.

'What we are saying,' said Henrietta quietly, 'is that

he is also from a different dimension from this one. And that makes everything much more dangerous.'

9

Up in flames

I woke up the next morning stiff all over and with various bits of me hurting more specifically. I tried to convince myself that I'd dreamed the weird trip to the Powerhouse. But my 'ordinary' everyday life was now more peculiar and unbelievable than any dream, so I failed dismally. I wondered whether to get Mum to write me a sick note. I certainly felt groggy enough to stay off school.

My parents were particularly kind to me that morning. Part of that kindness was letting me eat a bowl of cereal on the sofa while Dad played the video he'd made of last night's coverage of the demo. Have you ever seen yourself on TV? I thought I'd really made progress in the last few weeks; it had been ages since I'd thought of myself as ordinary and I suppose I expected it to show on the outside. It didn't.

We watched the marmalade-haired reporter valiantly commenting through the gloom as the demonstrators assembled. Then we saw the arrival of Bliss.

I looked really closely to see if he appeared strange or demonic, but whatever I'd sensed the night before wasn't visible on the TV screen. It was quite true that the fog thickened around him, but the average viewer wouldn't have seen that as anything supernatural.

'Terrible weather, wasn't it?' commented Dad.

'Yes,' said Mum. 'Only half our class turned up last night.'

The crowd surged forward. I glimpsed the Power family surrounding Bliss. Then there were shouts and scuffles and the picture started weaving around. I saw Mrs Everett go down, blood streaming from her forehead in a much redder flow than I remembered (perhaps we had the colour turned up too high on our set). Suddenly the camera veered round to an excited wild-eyed child yelling:

'Portland! Mrs Everett's hurt!'

My parents turned to me simultaneously and gave me mirror-image proud looks. I was horrified. That runt with the mousy, dishevelled hair was me. Portland's huge frame filled the screen, and then the camera pulled back to show the romantically-injured Eleanor lying limp in his arms. Her jacket clashed horribly with his beard.

'Ambulance!' roared Portland and the commentary stopped abruptly. There was a bit more footage of the demonstrators bashing one another and a shot of Mrs

Everett being helped into the ambulance. The newsreader in the studio said that about a dozen demonstrators had been treated for minor injuries at the local hospital but all had been sent home.

'Thanks to the alertness of one of her pupils, the teacher whose dramatic rescue you just saw, received only three stitches to a scalp wound. A hospital spokesperson said, that had she remained much longer in the mêlée, her injuries could have been much more serious.'

'Mêlée' was a very grand word for the undignified scene we had just witnessed. The AGOG! members had looked like football hooligans. There had been very clear shots of Dave and his friends, who looked like hooligans even when they were standing still – and they had been kicking and punching with great gusto. If Bliss had really engineered the violence, he'd succeeded in doing the library campaign considerable harm.

'Well done, dear,' said Mum. 'You certainly saved that teacher of yours.'

'It was Portland, really,' I said.

'Don't be modest,' said Dad. 'Mr Power was the brawn, but you were the brains. Quick thinking on the field of battle, that's what a good campaigner needs.'

'Yeah, well, perhaps I'll just join the army,' I said ungraciously. Now I'd seen myself on TV, looking so completely sad, I felt even less like going into school.

I was trudging gloomily along the road with my heavy bag of books ('You know we don't write sick notes when you're not really ill, Emily') when pounding feet came up behind me and Daniella thumped me on the back.

'Hi, Em! I saw you on the telly. I wish I'd been there, but my Mum said it was too cold. I bet it was brilliant!'

'Not really,' I said, but I couldn't convince her that it hadn't been a sort of cross between Hollyoaks and Heroes. At the moment it felt to me more like Torchwood, but I could hardly tell her that. She chattered happily all the way to school, as if we'd been just as friendly in the past few weeks as we had all our lives. I told you Dani doesn't bear grudges. She's actually very good at cheering you up and, by the time we reached the school gates, I didn't feel so bad. I almost told her about Joel's girlfriend but I didn't want to depress myself again.

There was a the usual mob of people milling around the gates, waiting for friends, talking about what they'd done the night before, borrowing other people's homework. When we approached a sort of cheer went up and they all surged towards me. I looked behind me.

'It's you, silly!' hissed Daniella. 'They all saw you on

telly too.' I wasn't exactly swept into the playground on people's shoulders but it was the sort of muted Elm Park equivalent of that. I could feel my face going red.

'You're lovely when you blush,' Fitzroy murmured in my ear and I managed to give him a good thump with my bag.

Assembly was a nightmare. Mr Risley, the headteacher, gave us a lecture on the dangers of mob violence and peer group pressure. Then he said: 'However, Elm Park students seem to have acquitted themselves well at the library demonstration last night, particularly Emily Grey, who behaved very responsibly and helped to save one member of staff from serious injury.'

Every head in the hall swivelled to look at me. That was the moment Eleanor Everett chose to make her dramatic entrance. She was wearing her palest make-up and a black suit with a frothy white shirt to match the snowy bandage wound round her temples. Spontaneous applause broke out as she took her seat at the side of our class, nodding coolly in acknowledgment.

I turned away to hide my smile. Mrs Everett *hated* assemblies and was expert at thinking up ways to get out of them. Often, she was with us when we set out for the hall, only to make her excuses somewhere along the route. But we hadn't seen her this morning. She must have come straight here. What a fraud!

At break-time, Archie got me on my own. The Powers had a plan to flush Bliss out. They were going to the newspapers with the bribe story, not just the local ones but then nationals. Henrietta was contacting the *Guardian* reporter who had done the interview.

'Couldn't that be dangerous?' I asked, 'If he's really what you think?'

'We have to find out,' said Archie. 'He was definitely acting like one of us last night.'

'But you said he wasn't on your side?' I protested, remembering the dreamlike discussion we'd had in the moonlight. 'What do you think he is?'

'He may be one of the ones who are after us,' said Archie.

'But how can he be?' I said. 'I mean, I never took much notice of local politics before the library thing but I *know* Alan Bliss has been around on the Council for donkey's years. I mean, we even went back to his house in 1983. He hasn't just arrived the way you did. Besides, if he'd come through the library, he wouldn't want to close it, would he?' My head was spinning.

'There is another possibility,' said Archie.

'What? That I'm going mad and imagining

everything, including you?' I snapped.

Archie didn't reply immediately. A cold feeling started in my stomach. I had been joking , in a masochistic sort of way, and I didn't want to be right.

'Leaving aside that possibility,' said Archie slowly. 'The real Councillor Bliss might have been invaded by another being.'

'What? You mean possessed. But why?'

'I think we have been … indiscreet in the use of our powers,' said Archie uneasily. 'I think we have attracted unwanted attention.'

'You mean that this being, whatever it is, has followed you here? Then why didn't it come the way you did, as a new person?'

'I don't know. None of us knows that. We don't even know if that *is* what's happened. But you must admit that Bliss seems different now from the first meeting.'

I thought of something else. 'Did the Majority Group meeting go ahead? Does anyone know what they decided?'

'They decided to vote to close the library,' said a voice behind us. Mrs Everett had come up behind us while we were talking. She was wearing flat-heeled Cossack boots, which is why we hadn't heard the usual tell-tale tattoo of her high heels. 'That creep Bliss came round to

144

my house with a huge bunch of red roses last night – God knows where he got them at that hour.' Mrs Everett tried to shake her hair, then remembered her bandage. 'Wolf was really quite annoyed.'

I boggled. 'Wolf' must be her husband! What a light it cast on her home life!

'What did he say?' asked Archie.

'He said, "I don't think my wife is up to receiving visitors,"' said Mrs Everett, giving a wicked little remembering smile.

'No, I mean Bliss,' said Archie, for whom Mrs Everett's private life held no fascination at all.

'He told Wolf to tell me how sorry he was that I got hurt,' said Mrs Everett. 'And he said to add, most particularly, especially since it was in a lost cause.'

'Did you keep the roses?' I asked.

She gave me a withering look. 'Of course I did.'

Then she seemed to remember she owed me a favour, or at least a nice smile. Anyway she let her glossy exterior soften a bit and said, 'I saw us both on the news, Emily, on the DVD.'

'Me too,' I sighed.

'You saved my life,' she said quietly and undramatically. I began to protest that it was Portland but Archie said, equally seriously, 'Yes, she did.' And I knew

145

that she was speaking from certain knowledge. Perhaps Fitz had done one of his sightseeing trips into the future and seen Eleanor's corpse or something? Spooky. The atmosphere was very heavy.

'Will you have a scar?' I burbled, trying to break it up.

'Only a small one,' said Mrs Everett, giving Archie a strange look. 'And it's under my hairline so it won't show.'

The whole library thing was dominating my life. I couldn't remember the last time I'd watched a silly TV programme, or read a fantasy novel or even rung someone up just for a chat. My world now was the AGOG! committee, the Powers, Friday night sleep-ins and planning tactics to defeat the Council. Oh yes, and I was in my first year of GCSE work too, not to mention violin practice and all the other little extras that school throws at you. I was getting like Mum, never to be seen without a clipboard and a list of jobs. But I felt more alive now than I had for years.

There was an emergency AGOG! meeting the night after the demo and my mother frowned as I got ready to go.

'It's all right,' I said defensively. 'I've done my homework – at least, I've done what has to be in tomorrow.'

'But you're looking peaky, Emily,' said Mum. 'It can't be good for you to be working on the library every night. You came home exhausted last night and it was quite dangerous by the look of it.'

'Mum,' I said, 'you weren't here when I came home last night. You never are. You're always at an evening class. And you're looking pretty peaky yourself.'

I didn't stay to see if I'd got away with it. If Dad had been there, I wouldn't have. There would have been mutterings about being cheeky and bad influences, which would have meant the Powers and the way Archie and her parents talked to one another as equals. As it was, I just heard Mum shout, 'Make sure they give you a lift home!' as I ran down the path. I hadn't actually slammed the door but I was giving a pretty good imitation of a moody teenager.

* * *

The mood at the Powerhouse was a bit volatile too. Not all the committee members had managed to get there, including Dad, but the ones who were there were pretty gloomy about the campaign's image after last night's débâcle. Henrietta soon changed that. She told them about the evidence we'd collected from the past – was that only last Friday? – and about her telephone conversation with Louise Somerville, the *Guardian* feature-writer. Mrs Everett was flushed with excitement under her white bandage.

'We've got them on the run,' she exclaimed. 'He'll never be able to authorise closing the library now we know that Strong is blackmailing him.'

'Unfortunately we don't have a copy of his letter to Strong,' said Henrietta, 'but we have seen it, at least, my son Albemarle has seen it.'

Fortunately no-one asked too many questions about how Albemarle had seen and memorised a highly sensitive and confidential letter, or how the Powers had got hold of damaging evidence of Bliss's dealings in the eighties. The meeting broke up early on a cheerful note. Wolf Everett came to collect his wife in a silver BMW. His hair was an even paler gold than hers, almost the colour of the car. He handed her into it like a duchess. I got a lift home from Portland in the psychedelic van, which looked just a tad tawdry compared with the Everett's car, particularly since I half felt it didn't really exist. It had just manifested itself in my universe along with the whole family of Powers.

'Hold on, Emma Leigh,' said Portland in my head. 'You have to keep believing just a little longer.' I gave him a startled look.

Next morning, all hell broke loose. I was at school with Archie, in the library. We had a free period and were helping Mr Yates the librarian unpack some new books. (He wasn't a patch on Joel, but he wasn't boring either – he wore leather jackets and was a whiz with any kind of technology, though he didn't seem terribly interested in books. I suspected him of being a secret role-play-gamer.) Luckily it was near the end of our free. Archie suddenly froze - as if listening to a transmitter implanted in her head. She grabbed my hand we were off without a warning. I'm not sure if teleporting or telekinesis is worse. In both cases you're being transplanted by someone else's will and power – at least you are if you're me. Teleporting might be OK if you did it for yourself. Anyway I found myself on the Powers' living-room rug, looking down at a shiny pair of black shoes. I was concentrating so hard on not decorating them with my breakfast that I couldn't guess who they belonged to.

'Ha!' said a nasty voice. 'I see you no longer mask yourselves! Or do you think the idiots in this dimension believe that all New Zealanders can fly through hyperspace?'

'Councillor Bliss,' came Henrietta's controlled voice. I lifted my throbbing head to see the bald little man standing on the rug a foot away from me, waving a newspaper and glaring round at the assembled Powers. They were all there. Archie led me gently to the sofa and let me sink into its brilliant throws and cushions. I closed my eyes; I could have done with a bit of beige tweed.

'We thought we should all be here to meet you,' said Henrietta.

'And the sickly one?' sneered Bliss. He actually raised one side of his lip at me. Elvis Presley he was not 'Is she one of you too? She doesn't look anything special. Is she going to help when I sue you for libel?'

'It's not libel,' said Lisle. 'We have the evidence.'

'Show me,' said Bliss.

It went very quiet in the room. You could hear squirrels scrabbling in the leaves outside the long windows. The Powers were communication telepathically so fast I couldn't tune in. I couldn't tell what Bliss was thinking; he had the telepathic equivalent of an electric fence round his mind. But I knew the Powers were evaluating the danger. Henrietta nodded to Fitzroy and he went over to the roll-top desk and took out and envelope.

'Open it,' said Bliss. Fitz slowly drew out the pages we had travelled through time and space to find. 'Look at them,' said Bliss. Fitz's eyes widened.

'They're blank,' he said, showing us the empty pinkish sheets.

'Illusionism,' said Grosvenor. 'Cheap showmanship.'

'No,' said Bliss smugly. 'Inferior technology. That photocopier I had in the early eighties used specially treated paper. The print faded after a year or two. It was a cheap home model.'

We looked at one another in dismay.

'You'll be hearing from my solicitor,' said Bliss and swept out of the room, though at his height and with his limited charisma it was a bit of a dustpan and brush effort.

We all sort of slumped. Grosvenor seemed quite furious.

'I'm not going to let him get away with that,' he stormed, walking up and down flexing his fingers.

'Careful, Grosvenor,' said Henrietta. 'Don't do anything rash.'

'Where's the harm if I do?' demanded Grosvenor. 'They know where we are now. That thing isn't human, is it?' (As if *he* was!)

'We'd better get back,' said Archie wearily.

'I'll drive you,' said Grosvenor. 'I don't think Emma Leigh could take another of your kind of journeys.'

As we drove along the almost deserted winter streets of Lark Hill Forest all the traffic lights turned green as we approached. As we turned into Elm Park Avenue, I gasped as I saw the school in flames. The fire alarm bell was clanging hideously and pupils were streaming out and getting into straggly lines.

'Quick,' I said. 'Let's get in before they find we're missing.' Archie gave me an odd look, but I jumped out of the van, dragging her behind me. We arrived at the end of our form line, out of breath and coughing from the smoke billowing out of the main building. 'How could it have happened so quickly?' I asked Archie. 'We can't have been gone half an hour.'

'I wonder,' said Archie, looking dubious. 'Cheap showmanship?'

'What?' I gaped stupidly.

She nodded over to where Grosvenor was leaning against the school gates, calm now, studying his fingernails.

'Illusionism,' she whispered. The she turned and mindspoke to her 'uncle'. I heard her. *Stop that immediately, Grosvenor. You'll frighten someone.*

I saw him shrug and sort of pull himself together, like someone claming down after losing their temper. As the fire-engine came screeching up the road with its siren blaring, I turned and saw that the school was no longer ablaze. Its bricks were not even blackened. There had been no fire.

10

Coming unstuck

If the teachers had been fazed by the sudden outbreak of fire, they were completely discombobulated by its equally sudden disappearance. The firemen were slightly annoyed but it was clearly not a hoax. Mr Risley himself explained to them there *had* been a fire; everyone had seen it. The chief fireman removed his yellow helmet and sniffed the air. The total absence of even a whiff of smoke puzzled both him and Mr Risley. The both went in to look over the building but I knew they wouldn't find their explanation anywhere there. Grosvenor sloped off back to the van and looked a bit sheepish.

'Wow!' I said to Archie. '*That's* a power and a half!'

She shrugged. 'We can all do it back home. Illusionism. That's how come we look like you.'

'How come it doesn't wear off the rest of you, if you've only got one power each?' I asked. 'No, don't tell me. It's just another of the things you don't know.'

Whenever I thought I'd got a handle on how the

153

Power family worked, it slithered away like mercury.

We were all shepherded back into school, where something even stranger was going on. Everyone was acting as if what had happened was a fire-drill. The fire-engine had gone and no-one seemed to remember the scarlet flames and choking smoke.

'That happens,' Archie whispered to me. 'If you perform an illusion in a dimension not your own, the inhabitants forget it – it's a defence mechanism, to preserve sanity.'

'What about the fog?' I whispered back. Archie shrugged. 'Perhaps that wasn't an illusion then. Perhaps the being that's taken over Bliss is a genuine weather-mage where we come from.'

Would I forget the Powers when they left? I didn't think so. But my mind was working on a way of using Grosvenor's newly-revealed skill to defeat Bliss. I don't think I learned anything at school that day. I was present in the lessons but nothing went in, not even English. My mind went round a well-worn track – must save the library, couldn't live without it, don't want to give up seeing Joel – ouch – change the subject – what could we do with Grosvenor's ability to create illusions? – would there be another sleep-in this Friday? – people already asking me – more and more people think it's important to save the library – can't live without it … etc.

I tried a few trips to the desert kingdom, just to get out of the loop. What would K'sedra, Empress-Mage, do? After all, I now had access to almost as many supernatural abilities as she did.

> K'sedra tossed her long shiny black braids and looked into her far-seeing mirror at her enemy. He sat, bald and smug, sunk in a heap of silken cushions.
> 'Hah, B'lys!' K'sedra said to his image. 'How am I to separate you from the demon that possesses you?'

It was no good. K'sedra probably wouldn't have bothered separating them – she would probably have had them both executed. I really wasn't cut out to be that ruthless, though I was sure the Powers could be.

Archie came and sat at my table at lunchtime. As she plonked down her tray, I could tell from the sparkle in her eyes that something new had happened.

'Crunch time,' she said. 'Tomorrow. The full Council meeting has been brought forward a week, to this Thursday. That's when the final decision's going to be made.'

I took it she had received a telepathic communication from home.

'This is it then,' I said. A fierce energy ran through me. I had one last chance to save Oak Grove and I was going to do it. 'I've got a plan,' I said. 'But it's going to take all of you together to make it work.'

Rumours flew round Lark Hill Forest over the next twenty-four hours. The library was saved. The library was doomed. Bliss was a crook. Bliss was the innocent victim of libel by unscrupulous fanatics. The library staff had received thirty-day redundancy notices. The book-fund had been doubled. Bliss was in prison. Bliss was in line for an OBE. The only thing we knew for certain was that the staff *had* received redundancy notices.

The library closes on a Tuesday afternoon and Isis and Joel had gone straight round to the Powers at lunchtime. They were still there when Archie and I came home from school. I changed into my jeans and sweater before I went downstairs to talk to them. Joel was leaning against the fireplace warming himself at the fire, as if he'd just come in from an arctic expedition instead of having spent the afternoon being cosseted by Lisle and Henrietta. Isis sat in an armchair looking equally numb.

'I never thought they'd actually do it,' she said and

I knew that she'd been saying the same thing, or variations on it, all afternoon.

'It isn't over yet,' I said. Joel gave me a beseeching look as if he really believed I *could* save his job.

'Best go home now and prepare for this evening,' Henrietta said gently. I knew she was getting rid of them but it didn't sound like it. She'd have made a good diplomat. I had permission from my parents to go to the Town Hall with the Powers and we needed the librarians out of the way while we talked tactics. The evening's events were going to take careful co-ordination. And one of the first things we had to do was steal Councillor Bliss's car.

The dream-van was packed with Powers that night. As it rattled and bumped over the ill-maintained streets of Lark Hill Forest there was a strong feeling of mutual purpose inside – I imagined this was how the SAS felt before a serious bout of yomping. And the brilliant thing was we didn't need walkie-talkies because of the telepathy. Portland parked a couple of streets away from Bliss's house and Henrietta stayed in the van. That was vital. We met Fitz outside Bliss's house. He had been hanging around a lamp-post across the road, making sure the councillor didn't leave early. We waited together in the circle of yellow light under the lamp-post. Unlike the night of the demo, it wasn't foggy, but calm and cold, the way it feels just before snow. It was nearly December.

'*Let's hold hands,*' someone said in my mind and we all reached out. If anyone had seen us we'd have looked like some weird outdoor alternative therapy group. But it felt comfortable. And then it began to feel more like switching on a computer and hearing the surge of power that lets you know it's up and running. Automatically I closed my eyes; I was beginning to feel *personally* powerful, shining with my own light – a sun not a moon at last.

'Quick, there he is!' hissed Archie and the circle was broken. Councillor Bliss was coming out of his door. He pulled on a furry hat and turned up his collar, turned back over his shoulder to say goodbye to his wife, then pulled the front door closed. He looked across the road and saw us but then the seven of us mindspoke: 'Henrietta, now!' and he vanished.

I found I'd been holding my breath, so I let it out slowly, making little puffs of steam in the cold night air. The next bit was going to be difficult. So far no-one knew exactly what Lisle could do, including her. I'd been through a list with Archie that was as bizarre as any conversation I'd had since she'd appeared that day in the library. It seemed that back in their dimension they all had skills which would be regarded here as the equivalents of making themselves invisible, controlling the weather, clairvoyance, telepathy with animals and the ability to reach into objects and beings and tinker around with what was inside. That was in addition to telepathy, which they all seemed to have, and the individual powers that each had manifested so far. Fitz's time-travel, Henrietta's telekinesis, Portland's shape-shifting, Archie's teleporting, Albemarle's X-ray vision and Grosvenor's recently revealed abilities as an illusionist. The list wasn't exhaustive; Archie ran out of her words or descriptions for what went on in her universe and I asked her to stop anyway. It always made me uneasy to think what they might be like where they had come from.

It was a long shot, but I was banking on Lisle having the ability to reach into Bliss's car and open the door. If she could, Fitz was going to plain old hot-wire it like an ordinary car-jacker. Of course, if what Lisle could do was communicate with animals or cause a hailstorm, that wasn't going to get us very far and I'd have to think again. But with the rest of the plan in place and most of the Powers around me, I was sure we could get into that car somehow.

I was wrong. Lisle and I strolled across the road and lingered round the councillor's red Nissan. I looked up and down the street, checking the front window of the house now and again, in case Mrs Bliss should look out. Lisle ran her fingers over the outside of the car. She had a frown between her bird's wing eyebrows; nothing was happening. I shifted from foot to foot. It was essential that we shouldn't be late for the Council meeting.

All of a sudden the Powers' van came screeching round the corner and a furious Councillor Bliss leapt out of it. This was all wrong. He came fuming over to us and for the first time I really began to believe he could be possessed. A positive smell of evil was coming off him.

'*What* do you think you are doing to my car?' he hissed at Lisle. 'Get out of the way. I have a meeting to get to and *a library to close*!'

We all stood frozen in our various positions: a winter tableau. Bliss unlocked his car and yanked the door open. The moment the engine started to purr, Lisle was galvanised. I felt the surge of power coming off her like the heat from a log fire.

Then all the doors of the car fell off. I don't know what she did to make it happen. It wasn't in the least bit funny. It was terrifying. Bliss sat, stupefied, as his car unmade itself around him. Glass fell out, chrome trimmings unpeeled, body panels came unsoldered, the whole thing was a reverse process of whatever had happened in the factory where it had been made. I daresay all the nuts and bolts and screws would have reverted to iron ore and alloys and the leather seats to cows if Portland hadn't rushed over and grabbed Lisle by the arm.

She was trembling with exertion and rage. Bliss stared open-mouthed, surrounded by the dislocated components of his car. And while he was stunned, Archie and Fitz made a grab for him.

'*Plan B,*' I felt them say, just before all three disappeared.

'Descolada,' said Portland, unbelievingly, as he held the spent Lisle in his arms. 'Who would have thought it?'

'What is it?' I asked. 'What exactly did she do?'

'There isn't really a word for it in your language,' said Grosvenor. 'Descolada is the word that comes closest. It's Portuguese.'

'It means unglueing,' said Albemarle. 'It's the power to unmake any made thing, to return it to its component parts.'

'Can you all do it?' I asked. 'I mean, could you? Before you came here?'

'No,' said the three brothers simultaneously.

'None of us could, not even Lisle,' said Portland. 'It's something rarely found even in our society.'

Lisle was looking at her hands as if they were loaded guns. I looked at the pathetic heap of metal and glass and plastic that was Bliss's car and realised we had a new problem.

'Can she put it back together?' I said. Somehow I knew, even without their solemn head-shaking, that there was no chance. 'What are we going to do?' I asked.

'We must just call on Grosvenor's powers a bit sooner than planned, that's all,' came a brisk voice. It was Henrietta, who had walked from where the van had been parked. She had a black eye.

'Are you alright?' asked Albemarle.

'Yes, yes, don't fuss,' she said. 'It's bad enough that I didn't realise a seventy-year-old human could be overcome by a fifty-year-old in this ridiculous dimension. Let's get on with it. Grosvenor, you'll have to make this heap of scrap look like a car again.'

I didn't think it would work. Grosvenor just looked at the bits and they started to lift off the ground and dance in the air. Gradually, a new car emerged from the whirlwind of bits. If you weren't paying closed attention, it *looked* like a red Nissan but if *felt* as fake as a new Beatles record.

'*I'm not going in that,*' I thought and the remaining Powers all laughed. I hadn't meant to send the message telepathically but nothing would induce me to ride in a vehicle that was just a collection of spare parts held together by Grosvenor's showmanship.

'It's all right,' said Lisle. 'I don't feel like getting in it either. We can go in the van. Are you ready, Portland?'

Then Portland began to shrink before my eyes. His red hair and beard disappeared and his head shone like a billiard ball. Grosvenor cast a bit more illusion over him and the grey overcoat and furry hat of Councillor Bliss completed the picture. The fake Councillor Bliss got into the fake Nissan.

'Good job he left the keys in!' said Portland in Bliss's voice, but he was joking. This was not going to move by anything other than supernatural means. Grosvenor and Albemarle handed Henrietta into the front passenger seat as carefully as if she had been their real seventy-year-old mother. Grosvenor passed a hand over the black eye and took the bruise away. Then the uncles got in the back and the 'unglued' car, incredibly started to move down the road.

'Come on,' said Lisle and we ran to the van.

'Do you think this is going to work?' I said anxiously and Lisle gave me one of her most bewitching smiles.

'Where do you think Archie and Fitz have taken the real Bliss?' I asked. It hadn't been part of the original plan to involve them at this stage.

'Does it matter?' asked Lisle, concentrating on the road. 'Somewhere far away and long ago preferably.'

'Can you do the ... the ... 'descolada' to people?' I asked. Lisle suddenly seemed an awfully dangerous enemy.

'It is forbidden to do it to any living being where I come from,' said Lisle. 'It is only the made that can be unmade. That is our law, but obviously it could be disobeyed.' I had a vision of Bliss in bits and suddenly thought I might be sick. 'It's all right, Emma Leigh,' said Lisle. 'We're not killers. But we *are* fighters.' There was a glint in her eyes as we drew up outside the Town Hall.

'Ah, there you are!' said Mrs Everett, coming forward to meet us. She had replaced the bandage with a sticking plaster and had her fine blonde hair cut in a soft fringe that fell over it. 'Everyone's been asking for you, Emily.'

An impressive crowd of protesters had been gathered at short notice. All the Elm Park lot were there and, since it was a clear though chilly night, some of the older Oak Grove supporters had come too.

'Bliss should be here any minute,' said Mrs Everett, consulting her watch. Lisle and I exchanged conspiratorial looks.

'There he is!' shouted one of the protesters, who knew Bliss's car. The red Nissan drove up and Bliss got out, accompanied by a woman and two men who looked vaguely familiar. I watched Eleanor closely but she didn't say 'What are the Powers doing in his car?'. In fact, after Bliss had gone into the Town Hall, she asked me where Portland was.

'I think he might be inside,' I said truthfully. There were a limited number of seats open to the public at a full Council meeting.

'We'd better get in then,' said Eleanor. We managed to slip into the seats Isis and Joel had saved for us, just before the mayor took his chair. I wasn't sure if Lisle had followed us in but I could see Henrietta and the uncles, even if they did manage somehow to look like Bliss's secretary and bodyguards respectively. I wondered if Grosvenor could really carry it off.

I was pretty sure Portland could sustain his new appearance indefinitely, but Grosvenor was having to keep together an unglued car that was out of sight and created the illusion that he and two other Powers were unlike their usual selves. We'd also agreed that he'd keep an eye on Portland and if anyone questioned his impersonation of Bliss, Grosvenor would come to his aid. But as Portland sat there fussing with his briefcase and taking the top on and off his pen, I couldn't see that anyone would doubt him.

The agenda was huge. Councillors droned on for ages about cuts here and savings there. Finally we got to the item about leisure facilities and the budget. The Leader asked Bliss to talk about finances. I don't know whether what Portland said made any kind of sense. Everyone was nodding, but that could have just been Grosvenor's influence. But at the end Portland said very clearly: 'I am happy to inform Council that extra money has been found in the contingency fund which means we can avoid the painful necessity of closing one branch library. Consequently I am pleased to inform you that Oak Grove library will remain open for the foreseeable future.'

A cheer went up from the gallery. Joel and Isis embraced and then, joy of joy, both gave me a hug. Even Eleanor Everett who claimed to be 'the least touchy-feely person in the universe' briefly brushed her scented cheek against mine.

The mayor had to call the meeting to order. I waited just long enough to see Bliss's words minuted, then sneaked out of the Council Chamber. I needed to be by myself. A rather bored security officer was standing in the car park having a smoke. I stood in the cold night taking deep breaths and trying not to inhale any of his nicotine. Then I heard him exclaim 'What the …?' I turned and saw the Bliss's car was coming apart. At the same moment Archie and Fitz materialised in the car park, and, clutching the ends of Fitz's army great-coat, was a very angry Councillor Bliss.

11

Celebrations

Bliss let go of Fitz as if he was red-hot and stormed over to me. 'Don't think I don't know you're behind this!' he snarled. He paused only to point a finger at the guard, which left him standing frozen in gormless amazement as Bliss swept past him into the Town Hall. The ordinary Councillor Bliss couldn't have done that; we really were up against something more than human now. I could see what was going to happen – two Blisses, the decision revoked, the imposter revealed, the police called – that is if everyone wasn't driven mad by the sight of Bliss and his doppelganger in the Council Chamber at the same time.

A cold calm settled on me and my whole being became one big NO. I remembered the warm hug from Joel and the spicy scent of his tickly woollen jumper pressed against my nose. I was not going to let Bliss take away the sweet victory of saving Oak Grove.

'Portland, he's back!' I said mentally and: 'Grosvenor, the car's coming apart,' although I was worried that he wouldn't be able to handle both crises at the same time. Archie and Fitz were with me, out of breath and humiliated by Bliss's escape.

'We took him to Antarctica,' said Fitz, teeth chattering, 'before there were any explorers there, but he grabbed me as we were leaving.'

'Well, what did you expect?' I asked crossly, as we ran. 'It would have killed him to stay there. You didn't have to be so extreme. Last week in this car park would have been enough.' Actually I was beginning to doubt that even the two of them together could be a match for whatever had taken hold of Bliss.

We were running to catch Bliss up. He was only a few yards ahead of us when the door to the Council Chamber swung outwards and he suddenly came face to face with himself. But not for long. One short, bald, middle-aged man grew and sprouted fiery hair and a beard as Portland reappeared in all his Viking splendour. The other remained as he was, unimpressive, but extremely malevolent.

'Quick,' I said, grabbing Fitz and Archie, 'take me back to Bliss's study, the moment after we left with the photocopies.'

We whirled off and I was buoyed up with my determination that I hardly felt a jolt when we arrived in

Bliss's study of 1983. I had the uncanny sensation of air whistling past me, as if our previous selves had only just departed through hyperspace and we'd missed them by a whisper. But I *didn't* have a headache and I headed straight for Bliss's hiding-place. 'This time we're taking the originals,' I said, taking no notice of Archie who was trying to protest. She exchanged looks with Fitz and they both shrugged. 'Come on,' I said, as soon as I had the evidence. 'Back to the Town Hall, the exact moment we left it.'

But that can't quite be done, there's always a slight dislocation of time and space, even if it can only be measured in microseconds and tenths of millimetres. That's what's so disorientating.

I rocked on the balls of my feet as we arrived back and found Portland and Bliss still glaring at one another. But Bliss knew something was wrong. He turned and stared at me uneasily. His overcoat and hat were wet with melted snow and I felt almost sorry for him, at least for the old Bliss. It was as if the real man, who was still in there somewhere, was asking me to rid him of the intruder that had taken over his body.

'You can't change the decision,' I said, my heart thumping. 'I've got the evidence of your dirty tricks.' I held up the paper, just out of his reach. Bliss looked trapped, as well he might, surrounded by three supernaturals and one completely obsessed and desperate human. I swear he ground his teeth as he pushed past us and out into the car park. As Bliss walked past, the guard slumped. The councillor took one look at his demolished car, now strewn in pieces around the car park, then turned on his heel and walked off. But I didn't think we'd seen the last of him.

The security guard sat up and moaned. He looked at the heap of car bits with the expression of a man who knows he's going to be asked how that could have happened while he was on duty. We were all watching.

'Couldn't Grosvenor do anything about it?' I asked. Portland shook his head.

'Probably too busy keeping everyone thinking I'd just slipped out to the loo.'

'Well, you'd better get back, hadn't you?' said Archie.

'Yes, we have to see this charade through to the end,' said Portland. 'Well done, Emma Leigh. Only I hope you don't have to pay too high a price for your ingenuity.'

'What does he mean by that?' I demanded, as Portland shifted back into the far less prepossessing shape of Councillor Bliss and re-entered the Chamber. Suddenly, the time-and-space-travel round trip caught up with me and I found my knees going wobbly. Fitz sat me down in a chair and Archie got me a bar of chocolate from the dispenser in the Hall's grand lobby.

'Eat this,' she said firmly. 'Your body sugar's suffered a big drop.'

'What does he mean?' I repeated doggedly, letting the sweet chocolate dissolve on my tongue.

'He means,' said Fitz, 'that you brought something from the past to this time. That can upset the balance, you know.'

'But we did that last time,' o objected. 'We brought the photocopies back, even though they were worthless.'

'I'm not sure how it works,' said Archie. 'But they were something we made, a duplicate of what existed back then. It doesn't have the same effect.'

'But we didn't make the paper, did we?' I said. 'And we brought that back. I don't see the difference.'

'Let's hope you don't,' said Fitz, gravely for him.

I was getting distinctly uncomfortable. All this evening I had been finding it difficult to distinguish myself from the Powers. I was beginning to feel as if I could *do* things myself, impossible things, the sort of things I'd previously only been able to do when I was pretending to be in the desert kingdom. That was it. When I was K'sedra I was pretending. Only now I wasn't. In spite of exhaustion from my quick trip into the eighties, I was still tingling and fizzing with power. The Council Chamber door opened again and a heap of Oak Grove supporters poured out, Eleanor in front.

'Ah, Emily,' she said, 'slipped out for a quick chocolate jag, did you? I don't blame you. I feel quite *drained* myself. I'm off to the pub. Anyone coming?'

Most of the spritzer set had been in the gallery and they all flowed down and around us. The library bit of the agenda was over but Portland would have to stay mimicking Bliss to the bitter end. Sometimes it was no fun being from another dimension.

'I don't think we should go to the pub,' came a clear voice of Gabrielle Connell. 'Emily can't come with us if we do. Let's go to the Coffee Bean instead.'

Mrs Everett made a little moue of distaste. But she quickly recovered herself. 'Quite right, Gabrielle. We must have Emily.' She struck a pose. 'For her I shall forswear alcohol – but only for tonight. Come along.'

We swarmed along the High Street, exhilarated by victory.

'Pity about tomorrow's sleep-in though,' said Jacob, giving Gabrielle a lascivious look. I wondered if anyone would ever look at me like that.

The Coffee Bean's owner, Phil, was a bit surprised to get so many customers all at once; we practically filled the café. Joel and Isis had come with us too. Lisle had come out to join Archie and Fitz and me, but all the other Powers were still at the Town Hall. Mrs Everett kept asking after Portland. She seemed to have developed a soft spot for him since the night of the he-man rescue. When we all had our drinks, she proposed a toast in cappuccino.

'To Oak Grove Library and all who slept in her!' she said.

'Oak Grove,' we all murmured in that indistinct way people always do with toasts.

'How can you drink that stuff, Emily?' Mrs Everett asked, looking incredulously at my lime milkshake. It did look rather bilious.

'Are you all right, Emma Leigh?' Archie whispered to me. 'You look about the same colour as your drink.'

'I don't know,' I said. 'I've been feeling a bit peculiar ever since we fetched the papers.' I felt in the pocket of my jacket; they were still there. Fitz and Archie exchanged worried looks. 'What?' I asked. It was disconcerting to have them watching over me for symptoms of a condition as yet undefined. 'What's going to happen?' I demanded, under the hubbub of conversation from the Elm Parkers. 'Am I going to sprout wings or and extra head or something? If I'm going to change I wouldn't mind being three inches taller or fabulously beautiful, but I don't suppose that's on offer?'

'Don't joke about it, Emma Leigh,' said Fitz. 'You are quite beautiful enough already.' There had been a small window of silence in the chat and everyone heard him say that. A chorus of laughs and whistles followed and I blushed all over. I noticed a furious Daniella glaring at me from the next table. I knew it wasn't just that she fancied Fitz herself, although she did. She was annoyed that I hadn't shared my secret with her, as I would have done in the old days.

'*If only you knew,*' I thought. '*I'm not having a thing with Fitz. I'm trying to get him or any member of his weird extra-terrestrial family to tell me what supernatural fate I'm about to suffer!*'

My powers of telepathy must have been increased, because Daniella gave me a really startled look.

'*Don't worry,*' Archie mindspoke. '*She won't understand even if she received your thought. But it's better not to telepathise with anyone other than us.*'

Into a third round of coffees and shakes and self-congratulation, Lisle suddenly stiffened. No-one else noticed but she sent a thought to Archie and Fitz and me.

'The meeting's over. The others are coming.' I 'heard' it much more clearly than the other telepathic messages and what's more, I started to see in my mind, like a TV news report, pictures of Portland as Bliss walking out of the Town Hall flanked by the uncles and Henrietta. He walked over to where the Nissan had been parked and looked round quickly. There was no sign of the guard. The other Powers encircled him and the figure who stepped out of their midst was Portland again. All four of them walked over to where Lisle and I had left the dream-van. The image vanished. I looked at Archie and Fitz.

'Did you see that?' I whispered.

'You can see now as well as hear?' Archie asked, but she seemed worried, not impressed.

A little later, the door of the Coffee Bean opened, ringing a bell, as the four Powers came in. Phil came forward to find them some chairs.

'Ah, Portland, at last,' said Eleanor, as if the other three didn't exist. 'Where were you? We've been celebrating.'

'I was seeing Bliss safely off the premises,' said Portland truthfully.

'I didn't see you at the Town Hall,' said Eleanor frowning.

'But it was such a crowd, wasn't it?' said Lisle smoothly. 'I never saw him myself.'

'I ought to go,' I said, suddenly realising how late it was. 'My parents will be worried.'

'I'll phone them,' said Eleanor, taking a mobile

phone from her handbag.

'And I'll drive you,' said Portland.

'Oh, but you've only just got here,' pouted Eleanor.

'I can give you a lift too,' said Portland. 'There's plenty of room in the van.'

'No, thank you,' said Eleanor. 'As soon as I've called the Greys, I'll give Wolf a ring. He'll pick me up.'

The party started to break up. There was a lot more hugging and kissing, including another embrace from Joel. I felt quite suffocated as if I had to tell my lungs to breathe and my blood to keep circulating. It was a relief to get out of the warm fug of the café and into the cold night air.

'You must be the only person in the world who can get high on lime milkshake,' said Fitz, affectionately, putting an arm round me.

'I don't think it's milkshake that's doing it,' said Portland. All the Powers were standing around me on the pavement, sending thought-waves of concern over me.

'You can go now, any time you like, can't you?' I said. 'The library will still be your gateway.'

'We shall return when it is safe,' said Henrietta.

'You mean safe in your dimension,' I said.

'No,' said Lisle. 'Not just there. It must be safe here too, for you. Remember that the problem of Bliss has not yet been solved.'

But it was too much for me that night. I just wanted to go home and go to bed, though my mind was racing so fast I doubted if I'd sleep. I don't really remember the journey home. I *suppose* we all got in the van but all I can recall is a rushing sensation and being at my front door. I staggered into my parents' arms, saying:

'We won! We saved the library.' And then I don't remember anything till the next morning.

Although I slept heavily, I had terrible dreams that the library was not saved. In my dreams, the door of it stood like a flaming arch, through which I could see a swirl of lights and colours that I knew was the path to the Powers' real home. Over and over again, as I watched, the arch shrank in on itself till the opening closed up and disappeared. Every time the dream began again I knew I could stop it if only I could get close enough to the arch. And every time I stayed rooted to the spot, held back by the gross solidity of my human body. I longed to flow through time and space the way I had with Fitz and Archie, not bound by the restrictions of my ordinary everyday world.

My mother came into my room with a cup of tea. My head was aching and the light hurt my eyes when she pulled the curtains.

'White rabbits, white rabbits, white rabbits!' she said and I gazed at her, not realising what she meant. It was the first day of December. I sat up in bed, sipping my tea and thinking about the last five weeks. It would be Christmas soon. I'd have to start thinking about presents and Mum and Dad would soon start the annual discussion about whether to go to one or other set of grandparents or have them all to us.

Three more weeks of school. Would Archie and Fitz still be there next term? I doubted it. I was already aching with self-pity. Mum was sitting on my bed, scanning my face. I looked at the clock and nearly spilled hot tea all over my pyjamas.

'Mum! It's nine o'clock! Why didn't you call me?'

'It's all right,' she said. 'I've phoned the school. I told them you'd be in late, if at all. You really needed your sleep, Emily. You came in last night like a zombie. I mean, it's very well done about the library, but it's really taken it out of you. You must try to get back to normal now, or your health will suffer, not to mention your schoolwork.'

My schoolwork was hardly going to benefit from a morning's skiving off. But it was Friday and we had double games first, so I didn't argue.

I got up slowly, had a deep bath, ate a large plateful of toast and got my books together. The roads were very quiet as I set off for school, but I didn't go straight there. For some reason I just had to go to Oak Grove first. I kept thinking about my dream.

As I trudged along the cold street in my horrible Elm Park regulation pleated skirt, I was still Emily Grey, the ordinary girl who needed the library to escape into other, more exciting lives. But last night I had been Emma Leigh, someone with unexplored capabilities. Where was all that potential now? What could I do if a malign power was still intent on closing the Power's escape route? The library was the same for them as for me, only in my case it was a metaphor; in theirs it was a vital means of escape and return.

I walked up the steps to the library. The entrance looked reassuringly ordinary. I held the door open for a mother with a double buggy. The newspaper area was already full of old people shaking from the cold. Isis was on duty. She gave me an odd look.

'No school, Emily?' she asked, looking at my uniform.

'I've got a free,' I lied. 'I wanted to look something up on the way in.'

She leaned over the counter conspiratorially. 'I'm glad you've come though. Guess who's here?' She nodded in the direction of the main library. 'It's Bliss! I don't know

180

what he wants, but he's behaving rather oddly.'

My spine tingled. I moved towards the councillor with short steps, scarcely able to breathe or walk properly. He was still wearing his big overcoat although it was very warm in the library. He seemed to be carrying something underneath it. I came face to face with him by the Fantasy bay. He whipped round sensing my presence.

'Hah,' he whispered. 'If it isn't little Miss Save Our Library! You thought you were so clever, didn't you?' I saw he was dousing the books with petrol. He was obviously quite mad.

I wanted to call Isis but my mouth was dry. As if in a nightmare, I couldn't open it to scream.

Bliss came towards me, backing me into the Fantasy bay. Petrol slipped on the carpet and over my skirt. He took out a box of matches. I was going to die.

I didn't feel scared any more. Just very calm and very cold. Isis and the old newspaper-readers seemed a long way off. I could hear toddlers laughing and burbling in the children's library. The bookstacks on either side screened us from anyone else's view, but I was surprised that no-one had smelt the petrol It was strong and acrid in my nostrils. I felt, in a detached way, that it wasn't altogether an unpleasant smell. I had never minded being in our car when Mum or Dad filled it up at the garage.

Bliss took a match from the box.

'There is more than one way to skin a cat,' he said. I'd always hated that expression. Trust him to use it. I was right against the window, still unable to cry out. He struck the match and held it in front of him. I saw the flame and its reflection dancing in his mad yellow eyes. I knew that what was going to happen would be nothing like Grosvenor's illusion. This would be a fire that would destroy and hurt.

'No!' I said. A flood of energy coursed through me. I was not a victim any more. The grey carpet disappeared from under our feet and we were standing on warm sand. Bliss gaped and dropped the match harmlessly. Where the shelves had been were two rocky arms of a mountain's base.

I walked towards Bliss, my red velvet skirt swishing over the silver sand. I reached my hand into his body and encircled his heart.

'Avaunt!' I said, remembering Macbeth, and drew out a handful of something flickering and scalding. He fell to his knees, clutching his chest. Then there were two of me.

'I'll take that,' said the velvet-clad Empress-Mage and the navy-skirted schoolgirl passed the hot revolting thing to her. K'sedra released the vile fluttering object and it turned into a vast

bird of prey that soared away screaming, as a
hundred gold-armoured archers suddenly leapt
from behind the rocks and loosed their arrows
into the sky after it.

12

Memory

I came to and found Bliss unconscious at my feet. Little flames were leaping up around him. My tongue was loosed at last.

'Isis!' I screamed. 'Fire!' I made a dash for the extinguisher and covered Bliss and all the area around him in foam. The library was suddenly full of people. All the Powers were there and soon there were fire-fighters and paramedics too. It was a good thing there were or I'd have suffocated Bliss with foam. But I was sure he was dead already. Hadn't I plucked the heart out of him? (Or had that been K'sedra?) What would the inquest say? (And what was K'sedra doing there anyway?) Could I plead that I wasn't myself at the time? I was terribly confused.

'It's all right,' said a paramedic. 'It's not his heart. I think he fainted.'

'Not his heart,' I said stupidly. 'Couldn't be. Hasn't got one.'

The paramedic gave me a hard look and said to his

mate, 'You'd better give her the once over. She's in shock.'

But I was pronounced well enough not to need to go to hospital. All that was prescribed was sweet tea. Isis marched me off to the staffroom while Portland shepherded all the library-users out into the cold. Once Bliss had been loaded into an ambulance, 'Just in case', the fire-fighters took over the library and asked for it to be cleared. Only, somehow, none of the Powers saw that as applying to them. They all ended up in the staffroom too. So when Frank came to tell Isis the police had arrived, I was left on my own with the Powers.

'What happened?' asked Lisle.

I told them as best I could. It was a satisfaction to see them all so stunned.

'*You* did it,' said Portland. 'You separated Bliss from what possessed him.'

'I thought I'd killed him,' I said. My hands were shaking so badly I could scarcely hold the mug. Perhaps the paramedics were right.

'You sent the persecutor back too,' said Fitz, his eyes shining with genuine admiration. 'You saved us as well as Bliss.'

'It's time to ask her,' said Henrietta. They all nodded. I was still feeling other-worldly and couldn't follow what was going on.

'Emma Leigh,' said Archie solemnly. 'When the time comes, we want you to come, we want you to come back with us.'

'What? To your dimension? How could I?' I said.

'We can make it possible,' said Lisle. 'You have great powers. They were what helped us get here in the first place.'

'Think about it,' said Albemarle.

'You've always wanted to be different,' added Grosvenor.

They sat round the scarred wooden table whose white ring-marks were the ghosts of hundreds and hundreds of librarians' coffee breaks. They were all willing me to say yes, to go with them and leave Emily Grey behind forever. But the moment was broken by Isis. She had come to fetch me to tell the police my account of the fire.

'Don't be afraid to tell them, Emily,' said Isis firmly. 'They've got the petrol can and the matches and I've told them you would never harm the library.'

It took a long time explaining that I'd seen Councillor Bliss sloshing petrol and lighting a match before dropping to the ground unconscious. I left out the bit about how I thought he had intended to set fire to me as well as the books, and needless to say I left

186

K'sedra out of it entirely.

When they had gone I felt very empty. Isis was trying to phone the head of libraries. There would be no-one at home now and I couldn't face school yet. I wandered off down the maze of corridors back to the staffroom. Just before I got there I froze as I realised the Powers were talking about me.

'She won't come,' said Albemarle. 'I felt it.'

'Give her time,' said Portland. 'She may change her mind.'

'And if she doesn't?' said Henrietta.

'Then there's only one thing for it,' said Lisle. 'We'll have to erase her memory.'

'Why?' said Fitz. 'I don't see why. That'd be a cruel thing to do to Emma Leigh.'

Terror gripped me. They could do whatever they wanted.

'She's seen too much and done too much,' said Grosvenor. 'She couldn't return to ordinary life with those memories. *That* would be cruel.'

'I agree,' came Archie's voice. The traitor. 'Emma Leigh is too important to mess around with. She gave us a way to get here and she kept the way open for us to get back. We owe her everything. If she won't come with us, we must make sure her memories never allow her to regret it.'

A bleak choice lay before me. I must either leave my family and friends and go off into the unknown and become a collection of blobs of coloured light, albeit blobs with special powers, or stay behind and be Emily Grey for the rest of my life, without telepathy or anything else to keep me from being ordinary. I couldn't face them. I retreated back up the corridor and bumped into Isis.

'Ah, there you are,' she said. 'Your father's come to take you home. You're to spend the rest of the day in bed with a hot-water bottle and plenty of sweet drinks.'

It sounded a lot more attractive than ranging through hyperspace. It was just what I needed while I made up my mind.

The next day I had a surprise visitor. It was Bliss –I felt scared at first but what could he do? Mum and Dad were both at home. They weren't very keen leaving me alone with him but he said he wanted to talk to me in private. Mum went off to make him some coffee, leaving the sitting-room door open and Dad said he'd be next door in the dining-room working on some files. Bliss sat down heavily and studied his hands.

'I want to thank you for what you did,' he said. I said nothing. I was waiting to find out exactly what he thought I *had* done. 'I'm on bail, you know,' he said. 'As soon as I was discharged from hospital, the police arrested me for attempted arson. My solicitor thinks he can get the charges dropped, though. You know, a medical report saying I was under stress.'

'Not quite yourself,' I said, allowing myself a little smirk.

'No, indeed,' said Bliss. He looked at me properly for the first time. The madness had disappeared from his eyes. He was just a worried, rather seedy little middle-aged man. 'I don't know what got into me,' he said, 'but I do understand that you saved me from something.'

'That's OK,' I said awkwardly. 'Any time.'

'There's something else I'd like to say,' he said. 'That money. The five thousand pounds. I never spent it. I bought savings certificates with it and I've reinvested it twice since. It's probably worth almost double now.' He paused. I thought *'If you offer it to me, I'll shop you.'* I don't know whether he received the telepathic message but his next words took me by surprise. 'I knew it was wrong of me to accept the money,' said Bliss. 'It's always made me miserable. I never did anything like that before or since. I never told my wife. No-one else knows I've got it. When the certificates next mature, in about three years time, I'm going to donate the money to the library, to buy new books.'

He reached into his pocket and gave me a letter. It stated that the money held by Councillor Bliss in saving certificates would be donated to Oak Grove Library as soon as they matured. His signature had been witnessed by his solicitor. 'It's all right,' said Bliss. 'He doesn't know where the money comes from.'

'People are going to think it's because you were sorry for trying to set fire to it,' I said slowly.

'But I am,' said Bliss. I believed him. He looked absolutely miserable. I expect he also hoped this promise might get the arson charge dropped. But what could I say? He *had* been possessed when he tried to torch the library and, although he had no such excuse for taking bribes decades ago, he was obviously sorry about that. Councillor Strong had been almost as bad as him because he was willing to resort to blackmail. And ten thousand pounds would buy an awful lot of new books.

'It has to be an anonymous donation,' I said. 'No publicity.'

'Absolutely,' said Bliss. 'I'd rather my wife didn't know anyway. She's not a great reader.'

'Wait here,' I said and went up to my room to get the evidence of his sleaze. I gave it to him and he put his lighter to it. The danger of his being blackmailed in the future went up in smoke. At the first whiff of burning paper, both my parents appeared in a flash. I couldn't help it; I started to giggle.

The Powers were still with us at Christmas, but I knew they wouldn't stay much longer. We didn't talk about their departure but they did occasionally drop hints that the 'government' had changed. I didn't know how they knew and I didn't ask. There were lots of things I was never going to know, like *exactly* what they had done that had made them flee their dimension. But they had always said their world was not equivalent to mine and I wasn't going to waste any more brain power trying to understand it now.

My going with them did not come up again, so I guessed they had read my mind. My energies were concentrated now on blocking the Powers' access to my thoughts. You see, they don't know about this account and if I can hide it from them, even if they do erase this period from my mind, I can still get my memories back.

The Powers threw the most wonderful Christmas Party on Boxing Day. I think they'd all been reading up on Dickens; they gave a full-throttle Victorian Christmas. Of course, being vegetarians, there was no hogshead or goose but their house was fabulously decorated and there were gallons of spicy mulled wine and platefuls of delicious little savoury snacks as well as mounds of mince pies and slices of thick black Christmas cake. There had been a mild spell in the ferocious winter and we all took our mugs of hot wine out into the garden, where Grosvenor master-minded the most incredible fireworks display. I think *he'd* been reading Tolkien – I knew perfectly well that those rockets and roman candles had never come from our corner shop.

All the AGOG! people were there and lots of Elm Parkers, as the Powers said it was a celebration of our victory too. Jacob had brought his guitar and Albemarle somehow managed to play along on his flute. There were a few mad improvised dances as everyone got very mellow. I danced with Fitz who was looking fabulously handsome in a purple velvet jacket and ruffled shirt, which made up a tiny bit for seeing Joel holding hands with Catherine.

'She's nice, you know,' whispered Fitz in my ear. 'She's a bit like you.'

I blinked hard. I must defend my thoughts more carefully. I looked again at Catherine though and saw he was right. She did have pretty hair but she was no great beauty – just a nice, ordinary, sympathetic sort of girl. I'd always thought that Joel would go for someone stunning and special, because only someone special would deserve him. Fitz was definitely trying to tell me something. I was going to miss him.

Mrs Everett was dancing with Portland but she hadn't come to the party alone. Incredibly, the immaculate pale-haired Wolf was dancing with my mother. She sparkled up at him like a firework. I'd never seen her so animated. My dad was twirling awkwardly with Lisle in his arms and Isis seemed to be dancing with both uncles. Everyone was intoxicated and it wasn't just the wine. Daniella was in a bit of a clinch with Ryan Duffy and Henrietta was chatting up Frank. Archie came looking for me and drew me and Fitz into the kitchen.

'It's a good party, isn't it?' she said, pouring us some more wine.

'Brilliant,' I said. Fitz still had his arm round me.

'We'll miss you, Emma Leigh,' said Archie.

'I'll miss you too,' I said dutifully and meant it too, even though I knew there was a chance I wouldn't be able to.

'Let's drink a toast,' suggested Archie. 'To Oak Grove!'

'To Oak Grove!' we both said. And Fitz kissed me.

'I'll drink to that!' said Eleanor Everett, bursting in with Portland for more supplies of mulled wine. I had the strangest feeling that she had interrupted something important.

I got my parents to leave the party soon afterwards, though they were still enjoying themselves. Most people lived close enough to the Powers to walk home, which was perhaps why the wine had flowed so freely. It had certainly gone to Mum and Dad's heads and they walked home laughing, with their arms round each other. I could still taste Fitz's lips on mine, the spicy tang of the mulled wine, the sensation that I was about to lose myself. What would have happened if Eleanor hadn't interrupted?

Three years later:

The brown envelope flipped through the letter-box on the mat. I knew what it was. My novel, Daughter of the Desert *had found its way home from another publisher. I took the package up to my room, in no hurry to open it and read the rejection letter; I could guess what it said. 'Shows exceptional promise ... over-ambitious ... derivative ... fluent writing ... would like to see your next ...' I had six of them already. But I had other problems on my mind at the moment. Elm Park had been asked to provide material for the time capsule to be buried in the foundation of the new library extension being built at Oak Grove. As editor of the school magazine, director of the school play and general right-hand woman of Mrs*

194

Everett's, I had been given the task of drawing up a shortlist. 'Perhaps I should just bury my novel?' I thought.

I could ask Joel for help the next time I go to babysit for him and Catherine. I could call in on him in the group of portakabins which is housing the library till the new bit is finished. But then I'd be late meeting Felix in the Coffee Bean.

'I'm off now, Mum,' I called as I left the house and ran down the street.

Felix was waiting outside the café. He shoved his book in his back pocket, put his arms round me and gave me a welcoming kiss. We are almost exactly the same height and our hair is the same colour and almost the same length.

When we got inside, a voice called 'Hi Emma Leigh!' from the back.

It was Daniella. She had left Oak Grove after GCSEs and I hadn't seen her much recently. She had been working at the local travel agent and I had been caught up in A-levels, and in Felix, who had arrived at about the same time as Daniella left. From the moment he had walked through the gates of Oak Grove, my whole life had changed.

'Hi,' I said. 'You know Felix?'

'Yes, hi,' said Daniella. 'Do you remember Ryan?' The guy she was with did seem vaguely familiar. I seemed to recall a Ryan in the fifth-form. I think he left round about that winter when I got so ill, after we saved the library.

'Hi,' he said. 'You used to be called Emily before. And you were a lot shorter.'

Everyone laughed. I was used to being teased about my growth spurt. Everyone at school said I'd been stretched when I had all those months off with glandular fever.

'You came on all those sleep-ins at the library, didn't you, Ryan?' asked Daniella.

'Yeah, you bet,' said Ryan. He was quite nice-looking, though not my type. His hair was too short and he had a nose ring. 'I was quite choked when my Dad changed his job and we had to move away. Dani and I were getting on quite well by then.' He gave her a soppy grin. 'Anyway, I'm back now. Dad's been transferred back to Lark Hill Forest and Mum never really liked the new place.'

'This library thing was important, wasn't it?' asked Felix. 'I mean, I've heard a bit about it, the demos, the sleep-ins and so on.'

'Yeah,' said Daniella. 'The whole school was caught up in it.'

'Well, isn't there something from that time that you could use for your time capsule?'

'That's a good idea, Felix.' I seemed to remember that Daniella and Ryan had both joined the library campaign, even though it had been an unlikely thing for them to do.

'Yes, we must have something left,' said Daniella. 'Didn't we have sashes or something saying "Save Our Library"?'

'I've got a badge at home somewhere,' said Ryan. 'It says "A gig", or something.'

'AGOG!' I said, with a vague memory that I'd given him that badge. 'That's what it was. The Action Group for Oak Grove.'

'Didn't you stop it burning down?' said Ryan. 'The creep that used to be on the Council tried to torch it, didn't he?'

I felt uncomfortable. 'He was stressed out. He didn't really mean to. He's been very supportive about the extension.'

'I still don't reckon we'd have got an extension if it hadn't been for Councillor Grey,' said Phil as he came to clear our cups. I drained my cappuccino.

Felix grinned. 'That's her Mum, you know.'

'No kidding?' said Phil. 'Valerie Grey, Chair of Leisure Services? Well, she's a better councillor than Alan Bliss ever was.'

We left the café and said our goodbyes; Dani and Ryan promising to search cupboards and drawers for AGOG! memorabilia. I told Felix I'd ask Eleanor and Joel too.

'And I'll write to Isis,' I said. 'She was the other librarian, the beautiful black one, who went to live in New

Zealand.' I shivered, although the day was warm.

'What's the matter?' asked Felix, putting his arms round me. 'Someone walk over your grave?'

There was something about the library campaign, something to do with New Zealand, but I couldn't remember what it was.

'I'd better go home now, Felix,' I said. 'I'll see you later.'

When I got home, I opened the publisher's letter and decided to put Daughter of the Desert in my bottom drawer. Metaphorically speaking. I dragged my desk chair over to the wardrobe and climbed on it. I wanted to put the manuscript into the cardboard box where I keep my old school papers. Then I suddenly though I might find something in it about the library campaign.

I took the box down from the top of the wardrobe and lifted out some old essays. Underneath them was a notebook, with astrological symbols on the cover. I had never seen it before, but when I opened it, I saw the white pages were covered in my handwriting. It was dated three years ago, back in the time when I was still Emily.

I propped my back against the bed and read. It was fantastic stuff, a better piece of fiction than Daughter of the Desert, but why couldn't I remember writing any of it?

When I had finished, I brushed the dust off my fingers

and went down to the kitchen where Dad was preparing supper. He did most of the cooking now that Mum was so busy as a councillor, which was great, because he was much better at it.

'Dad,' I said, helping myself to raw carrot sticks. 'Do you remember when we were in AGOG!?'

'Leave those carrots,' he said. 'Of course. How could I forget? It's the only time I've ever been on a demo.'

'Do you remember a family called Power?'

He frowned. 'No, I don't think so.'

'On the committee,' I pressed. 'Who was the chair?'

'Wasn't it your English teacher, Mrs Everett?' said my father. 'She was very active in the campaign, I seem to recall.'

'You haven't got any old committee papers or anything, have you Dad? I'm looking for stuff to put in the time capsule for the new library.'

He shook his head. 'Sorry. I threw them all out. You should ask Mrs Everett.'

I decided to call Eleanor.

'Do you remember two students called Archway and Fitzroy Power? They would have been at Elm Park three years ago, when we were trying to save the library.' There was a pause.

'Fitzroy?' Eleanor asked. 'And Archway? They sound like roads in London. I'm sure I would have remembered *them. Why?'*

'Oh, just an idea I had,' I said.

'Well, what ideas have you had for the capsule?' asked Eleanor. 'We have to take it to the site next week.'

'I thought we could put in things from that time,' I said. 'You know, press cuttings, badges and stuff, our banners if we can find any.'

'Good idea,' said Eleanor, 'though you really must find a way of losing "and stuff" from your vocabulary. I'll put a notice on the board next Monday and see if anyone's still got any campaign ephemera. That's good local history thinking.' She put down the phone.

I was restless. I felt as a zombie-like as if I had been mind-wiped by aliens. Not that I believed a word of it.

'I'm off to the library, Dad,' I called. 'Won't be long.'

'Be back in time for supper,' called my father. 'We're eating at seven thirty.'

I raced down the road to Oak Grove library. It looked like a building site at the moment. The new extension works were so disruptive, some of the main library had been moved out. The car-park at the back was dotted with portakabins. One contained loos, one a sort of canteen for staff and three others held books. Some of the books were in store, but there was a rumour that an anonymous benefactor had given nearly twelve thousand to help re-stock the library. And that was on top of the large sum of money my mum, Councillor Grey, had got allocated for the extension.

The temporary library was closing for the day, but I got into the fiction portakabin before the doors were locked. There was no-one there but Joel, reading a book. When he saw me, he put his finger in it to mark his place and gave me a gorgeous smile. I remembered when that smile used to turn my heart over. Or did I? Was it just the influence of the notebook?

'Joel,' I said, out of breath. 'Have you heard of a novelist called Henrietta Power?'

'No, sorry. I can look her up on the computer for you, though. Is she a British writer?'

'No,' I said, 'She comes from a long way away.'

Joel turned off the lights and locked the portakabin door. He had shown no recognition of the name at all. We walked a little part of the way home together, companionably.

'How're Catherine and Fergus?' I asked.

'Fine,' said Joel. 'We're expecting you to babysit on Tuesday, so we can go to that Italian film at the Odeon. Is that still OK?'

'Yes, it's fine.' I said. 'Can Felix come too?'

'Course,' said Joel. 'Do you want me to look up Henrietta Power on the main computer when I'm next in Central Library?'

'No, it's OK,' I said, as we stood on the corner where

our roads home parted. According to the notebook, this was where I had been saved from robbery by a black panther.

I watched Joel walking off down the road, his book still in his hand. I took the notebook out of my pocket. There were a few blank pages at the end. I turned them, idly, and froze. Inside the back cover was a little paper cut-out man, stuck on with blue-tack. 'Ryan,' I whispered.

It all came rushing back, memory too strong for whatever the Powers had done to my mind. An image of Fitz's dark laughing eyes and wicked smile flashed through my mind, then faded. Everyone else might have forgotten them but not me, not any more. I was Emma Leigh now and I had Felix (although I'm sure they'd had something to do with that). I wasn't ordinary any more and now remembered how I'd found that out.

*　　*　　*

I think I'll start a new novel this weekend. But first there's something I have to finish. Then I'll put it in the time capsule.

Emma Leigh sat down on the little wall outside the library and took out her pen.

AUTHOR BIOGRAPHY

Mary Hoffman has written over 90 books for children that range from picture books to novels. AMAZING GRACE, commended for the Kate Greenaway medal, has together with its sequels sold over 1.5 million copies. The most recent title, PRINCESS GRACE, has been very enthusiastically received.

Mary has also written the highly successful teenage fantasy "Stravaganza "sequence, for Bloomsbury, which is set in an alternative Renaissance Italy. Her novel THE FALCONER'S KNOT, (Bloomsbury), a murder mystery set in the Middle Ages, was short-listed for the Guardian Children's Fiction Award.

For some years Mary has been living in rural Oxfordshire with her husband and three Burmese cats. She has three adult daughters who all work in the arts.

www.maryhoffman.co.uk

If you've enjoyed this book, you can find
more great titles from Barn Owl at

www.barnowlbooks.com

Barn Owl Books would like to thank, most profoundly, the following people, both friends and colleagues, who have generously made donations to the

BARN OWL APPEAL

The fund exists to keep Barn Owl publishing books and flying high in the literary skies, bringing the best of past writing into the present.

Marianne Adey

Pat Almond

Rachel Anderson

Lynne Reid Banks

Steve Barlow

Clive Barnes

Malorie Blackman

David Bradby

Theresa Breslin

Irene Breugel

Katie Brown

Louise Brown

Natasha Brown

Sarah Butler

Carousel Magazine

Jo Christian

Fred Crawley

Gillian Cross

Finette Deverell

Chris D'Lacey

Ruth & Derek Foxman

Frances Lincoln Publishers

Morag Fraser

Adele Geras

Nicola Gordon

Jim Gordon

Catherine Gordon

Lindsay Gordon

Andrew Gordon

Graham-Cameron

– illustators

Mary Green

Dennis Hamley

Kathy Henderson

Susan Himmelweit

Nigel Hinton

Mary Hoffman

Clodagh Howes

Julia Jarman

Mary & Bill Kennedy

David Kleinman

Richard Kuper

Liz Laird

Marilyn Malin

Anne Mallinson

Kara May

John McLay

David Metz

Gill Moorhouse

Michael Morpurgo

Beverley Naidoo

Linda Newbery

Jane Nissen

Linda Owen Lloyd

Kate Petty

Frank Rogers

Prof. Kim Reynolds

Hannah Sackett

Marsha Saunders

Susan Schonfield

Steve Skidmore

Angela Smith

Jeremy Strong

Howard Stirrup

Pat Thompson

Monica Threlfall

Elinor Updale

Peter Usborne

Miss A Walker

Bob Wilson

Dame Jacqueline Wilson

For information about Barn Owl Books or to make a donation please visit

www.barnowlbooks.com